*Get ready to be swept off your feet by perfect English gentlemen!*

Harlequin Romance® brings you another heartwarming read by international bestselling author

## *Jessica Steele*

Jessica's classic love stories will whisk you into a world of pure romantic excitement....

### Praise for Jessica's novels:

"Jessica Steele pens an unforgettable tale filled with vivid, lively characters, fabulous dialogue and a touching conflict."
—*Romantic Times BOOKreviews*

# JESSICA STEELE
*Her Hand in Marriage*

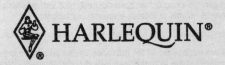

## HARLEQUIN®

TORONTO • NEW YORK • LONDON
AMSTERDAM • PARIS • SYDNEY • HAMBURG
STOCKHOLM • ATHENS • TOKYO • MILAN • MADRID
PRAGUE • WARSAW • BUDAPEST • AUCKLAND

ISBN-13: 978-0-373-17487-4
ISBN-10:   0-373-17487-X

HER HAND IN MARRIAGE

First North American Publication 2008.

This edition published by arrangement with Harlequin Books S.A.

® and TM are trademarks of the publisher. Trademarks indicated with
® are registered in the United States Patent and Trademark Office, the
Canadian Trade Marks Office and in other countries.

www.eHarlequin.com

Printed in U.S.A.

**Jessica Steele** lives in the county of Worcestershire with her super husband, Peter, and their gorgeous Staffordshire bull terrier, Florence. Any spare time is spent enjoying her three main hobbies: reading espionage novels, gardening (she has a great love of flowers) and playing golf. Any time left over is celebrated with her fourth hobby: shopping. Jessica has a sister and two brothers, and they all, with their spouses, often go on golfing holidays together.

Having traveled to various places on the globe researching backgrounds for her stories, there are many countries she would like to revisit. Jessica hadn't planned on being a writer until one day Peter suggested she write a book. So she did.

This is Jessica's eighty-fifth novel!

# CHAPTER ONE

ROMILLIE opened her eyes to a bright sunshiny morning and knew it was going to be a good day. Wrong! Well, perhaps not totally. Her mother, a poor sleeper, was already up and about when Romillie went down the stairs.

'Any plans for today?' Romillie asked gently. Eleanor Fairfax had suffered for some years with general low spirits and feelings of inadequacy, but of late there were more good days than bad.

'If this weather holds I thought I might do a spot of weeding or...' she hesitated '...I might take a sketchpad outside.'

Romillie's spirits soared. Her mother was a professional artist—portraits mainly. She was truly gifted but had not so much as picked up a sketching pencil in an absolute age.

'The forecast is good,' Romillie answered lightly, taking a quick glance at her watch and getting up and taking her cereal bowl over to the kitchen sink. 'Better be off. Don't want to be late.'

It was not far to the dental practice where she worked. But because she liked to return home in her lunch hour, and since her mother had given up driving, Romillie made the journey in her mother's car.

They lived in the village of Tarnleigh on the Oxfordshire and Berkshire borders. Her receptionist-telephonist job with Yardley, East, and—now—Davidson, was well within her capabilities. It was not a job she would have chosen to do, but it was convenient.

Five years ago she had intended to go to university. But everything had suddenly gone catastrophic at home. She had been coming up to eighteen, her place at university assured, when her grandfather Mannion, her mother's father and a man who had never had a day's illness in his life, had suddenly died.

She had been upset, her mother distraught. It had not ended there. They had always lived with Grandfather Mannion. Romillie's father, despite his frequent absences, had lived with them, too.

Her mother had adored Archer Fairfax and had put up with his womanising, his idleness, his spendthrift ways, making excuses for him whenever Grandfather Mannion would frown in his direction.

Romillie had known her father had other women. She had seen him driving along one time with a pretty blonde by his side. And another time, when he was supposed to be in Northampton for a job interview, and she had been in the school coach some miles from home after playing in an away game hockey match, she had seen him arm in arm, with a brunette this time.

He had returned home the next day, having not got the job but related that, after a very detailed and extensive interview, it had been felt that he was too well qualified for the job. Her mother had swallowed it all and Romillie just hadn't had the heart to tell her that he had been nowhere near a job interview.

But it became plain that Grandfather Mannion had been wise to his son-in-law in that when Archer Fairfax was of the opinion that he would now rule the roost, he discovered that his well-to-do father-in-law had left him not one penny. The bulk of his estate had gone to his daughter, Eleanor, with money left in trust for his granddaughter until she attained the age of twenty-five. The house, the large rambling house, had been left to Eleanor during her lifetime, or until she no longer required it, when it was then to be handed down to her daughter.

There had been shouting matches before, mainly Romillie's father roaring away when Grandfather Mannion was not around. But then, with no one there to keep him in check, Archer Fairfax had given his temper free rein. The consequence being that Eleanor, highly sensitive to begin with, shrank deeper and deeper into her shell. She lost heart, and gave up painting altogether.

Romillie had tried to intervene, only to discover that instead of helping she had made things worse. As a child she had suffered bouts of sleepwalking—but that had not happened in a long, long while. The last time had been on the night before she had been due to leave for university. There had been another tremendous row that night, her father yelling, drowning out her mother's cries of protest. Stressed and worried about leaving her mother with her bullying father, Romillie had gone to bed, only to awake the next morning to find that in her sleep she had got up and taken everything out from her suitcase. She knew then what she supposed she had known for some while—university, for the moment, was out.

One year passed, and then two, and things in the Fairfax household did not get any better. Her mother became more and more reclusive and leant more and more on Romillie. University seemed as far away as ever. Romillie thought about getting a job but did not know how she could leave her.

Grandfather Mannion's money kept them afloat for three years, but, what with Eleanor giving in to her husband's constant demands for money, at the end of those three years the money had gone.

When the money went, so too did Archer Fairfax. Guiltily, Romillie had been glad to see him go, but it was he who had brought her mother to the state she was in. For the next year they struggled on, Archer Fairfax appearing frequently, to make sure he was not missing out on anything.

And then out of the blue, one morning when Romillie and her mother were doing nothing in particular, Romillie had felt her mother's eyes on her and had the feeling that something momentous was taking place.

'What is it?' she remembered asking, certain as she was that she was picking up some pretty gigantic vibes.

Eleanor Fairfax had continued to look at her for some seconds more, and had then calmly enquired, 'I wondered, Rom, would you mind very much if I divorced your father?'

Wow! That *was* momentous! 'I'll get the car out and drive you to the lawyers, shall I?' she'd volunteered.

Oddly, once that decision had been made, Eleanor had seemed to gain some confidence. Archer Fairfax hadn't liked it, did not like losing control, but Eleanor had remained firm. She'd still had her 'off' days, but she was no longer at rock bottom.

She had not been able to resume her painting, though, and by then the need of an income had become a pressing need. Romillie knew then that university was definitely out. Instead she found herself a job.

She could probably have found a more interesting job, one that paid better, but that would have meant working further afield. And the chief bonus of working so close to home was that because of her mother's occasional 'off' days, she could return home at lunchtime.

There was another bonus, too. Jeffrey Davidson—her boyfriend. He was the new junior partner at the dental practice, a replacement for the soon to be retired senior partner. Jeff had been with the firm only three months, and she had been going out with him for two of them, which was a long time for her. She liked him, and believed she might even be a little in love with him. He was a good dentist, considerate to his patients and staff, and understanding when, because of her dislike of leaving her mother on her own for too long, Romillie seldom stayed out late. Her mother,

Romillie realised, seemed relieved and happy that she was 'seeing someone'.

So it was on that bright sunny April morning that Romillie parked her car and went swinging into the large old Victorian house that had been converted into a dental practice.

She stowed her bag behind the receptionist's desk and was taking her first call before she'd had chance to turn on her computer.

It was eleven o'clock before she knew it. Cindy Wilson, one of the dental nurses, came and took over while she went and made herself a cup of coffee. It was there that Jeff Davidson sought her out.

'I thought I might find you here round about now,' he said, his eyes admiring on her shining raven hair, now drawn back neatly, and looking deeply into her wide brown eyes.

'Sorry I couldn't make it last night,' she apologised, having cancelled their arrangement, though without explaining that her mother had seemed a bit down when she had gone home at lunchtime.

'No problem,' he replied good-humouredly. 'How are you fixed for tonight? We could go and see that new film.'

Romillie, recalling that her mother was so sensationally 'up' that morning as to actually consider picking up her sketching pad, smiled a warm smile. 'I'd love to,' she accepted.

Carrying her coffee back to her desk, she thanked Cindy for covering for her. But when Cindy did not go but fidgeted, moving things around on the desk, Romillie realised she had something on her mind. When she heard what it was, however, something in Romillie iced over.

'Are you and Jeff Davidson an item?' Cindy blurted out suddenly.

The dental nurse seemed wound up. Romillie, from experience, tried to help. 'Is it important?' she asked quietly.

'I went out with him last night,' Cindy said in another rush, and, while a sick feeling invaded Romillie's insides, 'I—um—wouldn't want to—um—you know, if…'

'Don't worry about it,' Romillie answered, somehow managing to maintain her quiet air. 'I have been out with him. But that's finished now.'

Cindy beamed at her. 'You didn't mind me asking?'

'Not at all,' Romillie replied, and even found a smile.

She carried on with her work, but all the while thoughts of the fickleness of men bombarded her. Her father was a prime example, and now the man she had been out with enough times to have begun to think of him as her boyfriend was another.

But, as she had told Cindy Wilson, that was now finished. If he thought she was going to the cinema with him that night did he have another think coming! All that remained was for her to tell him that.

Romillie went home at lunchtime, hid from her mother that she had received a pretty nasty jolt that morning, and ate the sandwiches her mother had prepared. She returned to work with a certainty that nothing would alter, that while she and Jeff Davidson might have been an item yesterday, they most assuredly were not an item today. Nor would they ever be.

She did not get the chance to tell him so until she went to make a cup of tea and he came to find her. 'What time tonight?' he began.

While the fear silently haunted her that she might have inherited some of her father's weaknesses, Romillie, with her years of experience of his dishonesty in his relationship with her mother, just knew without having to think about it that there would be no such dishonesty or underhandedness in any relationship she had.

'You went out with Cindy Wilson last night,' she said bluntly.

That caught him off-guard, but after a second or two he recovered. 'I didn't know I was yours exclusively,' he replied.

Romillie stared at him, her brown eyes wide and serious. Then suddenly she smiled. It was a phoney smile. She might be hurting but he would never know it. 'You're not,' she said. And, in case he had not yet got the message, 'Enjoy the film,' she bade him, picked up her tea, and walked away.

Romillie was still feeling churned up inside about Jeff Davidson when she drove home that night, and she blamed herself—when her father was a fine example of a two-timing man; in her father's case more than two timing—that she *had* believed that she and Jeff Davidson were exclusive to each other.

It made her angry that she had been such a fool. Once bitten twice shy, she vowed. And with her knowledge of her father's faithlessness, and now her supposed boyfriend proving to be little better, Romillie knew it would be a very long time before she trusted any man again.

She hid her hurt and disenchantment when she arrived home, and went in search of her mother. She found her in the kitchen.

'I saw you coming. I've got the kettle on,' Eleanor Fairfax announced, and seemed equally bright as she had at the start of the day, so that Romillie felt able to bring up the subject of her taking her sketchpad outside.

'Did you manage…?' It was as far as she got. For, guessing the question, her mother picked up the sketchpad from behind her.

'What do you think?' she asked, showing a small sketch of a corner of the garden.

'Mum, it's wonderful!' Romillie enthused, meaning it on both fronts. It was wonderful that her parent was showing an interest again, and her talent as an artist was truly wonderful too. Her attention to detail never ceased to amaze Romillie.

'Oh, I wouldn't go that far,' Eleanor protested. 'I might try painting it later, but I'm so rusty. I…' She left the rest unsaid, but was smiling happily as she revealed, 'I had a blast from the past this afternoon.' And when Romillie looked at her quickly, fearing the worst, 'No, not your father. Though no doubt Archer Fairfax will show his face again as soon as he wants something. No, I was absorbed in what I was doing when I suddenly felt someone's eyes on me. I looked up, and there in next-door's garden was Lewis Selby.'

'Lewis Selby?'

'You won't know him. I wouldn't have known him myself—I hadn't seen him in over forty years. He's a cousin of Sarah Daniels.' Sarah Daniels lived next door, but had closed the house up some months previously to go on an extended stay in Australia. 'Lewis and his family used to visit quite often when he was a boy—he'd have been about twelve the last time I saw him. I must have been five or six,' Eleanor broke off to explain, 'and I heard them having such fun in the garden next door that it seems I toddled off round there to join in. Lewis was delegated to take hold of my hand and bring me back.'

'You remember the incident?'

'Oh, I do. He was such a kind boy. Apparently I would look out of the window every day for him, but I didn't see him again.'

'Until today?'

'Until today,' her mother agreed with a smile. 'He knew from Sarah that I'd become an artist—was an artist,' she corrected. 'He didn't recognise me either, but came to the hedge when he saw me to make himself known.'

Romillie laughed. It was a joy to see her mother so 'up'. 'What a pity he didn't know that Mrs Daniels was away. Had he come far?'

'He lives in London and he knew Sarah was out of the country. She has been in touch, it seems, and guess what?' Romillie had no idea. 'Apparently Sarah, horse-mad Sarah, has met a man in the Outback—and won't be coming home.'

Romillie's eyes went wide in surprise. 'She's getting married?' she asked. Sarah Daniels, closer to sixty than fifty had, when widowed young, moved back to her family home.

Eleanor nodded. 'Isn't it lovely?' she exclaimed, seeming oblivious to the fact that marriage, as in her own case, was very often a disaster.

'Er—yes,' Romillie agreed, holding back from saying that now, and probably even before Jeff Davidson's careless treatment of what she had started to think was a little more than a casual association between them, she viewed the prospect of men and marriage through much less rose-tinted glasses. 'Um—so why did this—er—Lewis Selby visit if he knew she wouldn't be here?'

'Apparently Lewis is thinking of semi-retirement and Sarah contacted him with the idea of putting his semi-retirement to good use.'

'She's selling the house?' Romillie guessed.

'Not straight away,' her mother corrected. 'It seems that she and her Australian are mutually besotted and he's afraid that if she comes home she won't go back again. So to prove her love she has said that she will stay.'

'This Lewis Selby told you all about it over the hedge?' Romillie enquired.

'He started to,' Eleanor replied. 'But then I realised that all the services in Sarah's house must be disconnected. So, as I already knew him, albeit from around forty-four or so years ago, I asked him if he'd like to come round for a cup of tea.'

Romillie was little short of amazed—yet at the same time delighted. Her mother had not shown an interest in anything remotely social for at least five years! However, since the last thing she wanted was for her to retreat back into her shell, she hid her amazement and asked instead, 'So, the house isn't being sold just yet?'

'Sarah has a few very special pieces. Some she wants sold, others she wants shipped out. Lewis has a list, and was here today checking through and sorting out prior to contacting the valuers. Now, how about you? Are you going out with Jeff tonight and do you need an early dinner?'

It was good to hear her mother think about cooking a meal when for so long she had not been remotely interested in food. 'We can eat late if you like,' Romillie answered, pondering whether to say more but, with her mother so 'up', risking it. 'Other than work, I won't be seeing Jeff again.'

'You've split up!' Eleanor exclaimed, searching her daughter's face for signs of hurt, her own expression troubled.

'It was a mutual kind of thing,' Romillie answered lightly. 'I don't—um—fancy him any more,' she added, and knew as she said it that it was true.

She knew as lay in bed that night that it was probably because of her father chasing anything the slightest feminine that she had grown up being a little cautious where men were concerned. She had certainly been very circumspect with whom she went out with—which made Jeff Davidson so special that she'd gone out with him more than a few times. But, having dated him often enough to believe that they were sole boyfriend and girlfriend to each other, today's revelations had struck at the heart of her—and had killed stone-dead any feeling she might have thought she had for him.

Which, from his point of view the next morning, was rather unfortunate. Because no sooner had she arrived at her place of work than he was there, meeting her in the firm's parking area.

'Romillie.' He waylaid her. 'I was a fool. I'm sorry.'

She stared at him. Then she smiled—her phoney smile. 'Why, what have you done?'

'You've forgiven me?'

'Of course,' she said, still smiling, and would have walked on. But he caught hold of her arm, halting her.

'Prove it. Come out with me tonight. Let me show...'

Romillie looked pointedly down at his hand on her arm, and pulled out of his grasp. 'I think you must be confusing me with someone else,' she informed him coolly—and left him standing there.

The trouble was, she discovered over the next few days, that men were all casual and careless of your feelings when they thought you were interested, but once you had shown them that you were not remotely interested they just wouldn't leave you alone. Tough! She was not there to be picked up and put down again at the whim of Jeff Davidson, or anyone else for that matter.

He continued to frequently ask her out. She as frequently told him no. Her mind was on very different matters. Her mother was continuing to make progress. Slow progress, it was true, but after so many years in her private dark place, it was a joy to Romillie to see her picking up the threads of living again.

'I was wondering,' Eleanor mused as they sat drinking coffee after dinner one night, 'how you'd feel about sitting for me?'

Romillie could not believe it, but was more than ready to give her every encouragement. 'No problem,' she answered cheerfully.

As soon as his gifted daughter's artistic talent had shown through, Grandfather Mannion had had a studio made for her. And so it was that after her stint at the dental practice, where it seemed Jeff Davidson still had not taken on board that no thanks meant exactly that, Romillie would spend some part of every evening in her mother's studio while her mother re-acquainted herself with that which had once been her life.

It was during these sittings that Romillie learnt that Lewis Selby had been down, and had again been invited in for a cup of tea.

Indeed, as the weeks went by, it appeared that he came down once or twice every week and, out of courtesy, always knocked on the door to let her mother know that he was about. Out of that same courtesy, her mother would always invite him in for a cup of tea.

He was divorced, Romillie learned at one of their sittings. 'A rather acrimonious divorce too, I think,' her mother revealed. 'Though, because he's such a nice person, he never says a word against his ex-wife.' And, going on to another topic, 'How do you feel about doing a nude sitting? You needn't if you don't want to, but I'd like to try…'

'Happy to oblige,' Romillie answered. If her mother went on making progress like this she might soon be saying a permanent goodbye to her 'down' days.

At a further sitting Romillie learned that Lewis Selby had paid another visit, and had again been invited in. But when she privately wondered if he was perhaps interested in her mother, she discovered that he was seemingly still too bruised from his divorce to consider leaving himself open to anything like that again.

'It's nice that he can pop in from time to time,' Romillie commented lightly. 'Er—when does he retire?'

'Not yet. Not officially for another three years. He works for the telecommunications company Tritel Incorporated. But with him being chairman of such a vast company, it's not a job he can leave in an instant.' Eleanor broke off to concentrate on what she was doing for a while, and then resumed. 'Though from what Lewis was saying he has a very able deputy in Naylor Cardell, a man who, it seems, while dealing with his own work, is already taking on some of Lewis's duties. Keep your head still for a moment, there's a love.'

Romillie was in the kitchenette of the dental surgery a few days later when Jeff Davidson came in and tried a new tack. 'If I promise to keep solely to you while we're going out, would you bend just a little and come out with me again?' he asked. And as she just stared at him, because he *still* hadn't got the message, 'Did I hurt you so much, Romillie?' he went on. 'Did I? That you no longer trust me?'

Trust, in her book, was one very big word—and he had proved himself undeserving. She looked at him, tall, good-looking and with everything going for him—and yet he suddenly seemed totally without substance.

But her pride reared up at his question of whether his fickleness had hurt her, and there was no way she was going to let him know that hurt she had been, nor how betrayed she had felt.

And she who abhorred lies found in that proud instance that it was no effort to have a lie tripping off her tongue.

'I've moved on, Jeff,' she replied.

He cocked his head to one side. 'How?'

'Pastures new,' she told him without blinking.

'You're dating someone else?' he asked, seeming astounded.

'You seem surprised?'

'No, no.' He back-pedalled. 'You're very attractive… You know that you are. It's—um—just…'

It annoyed her that he should so conceitedly think she stayed home nights, hurting because of him. 'You blew it, Jeff,' she informed him coolly. 'Get over it.'

Her pride was fully intact when she drove home that night. But, when she went in it was to discover that her mother, who had recently been so up, looked tense, and had taken a step backwards.

'Had a good day?' Romillie asked cheerfully, starting to become convinced that her father had called and been up to his old trick of shattering her mother's confidence.

But it was not her father who was the culprit this time, but, surprisingly, Lewis Selby. And he was not so much shattering her confidence as wanting her to take a peep outside the safe little world she had made for herself.

'Lewis—called,' she answered jerkily as Romillie put the kettle on to make a pot of tea.

Lewis Selby had been there yesterday. Twice in two days! 'He must be nearly finished with his business next door,' Romillie remarked lightly.

'He asked me to have dinner with him!' Eleanor burst out in a sudden rush.

Oh, heavens! Romillie kept her expression impassive, but knew the answer even before she asked the question. 'Are you going?'

'No, of course not!' Sharp, unequivocal. And she saw that her mother, like herself, was a long way from trusting again.

Romillie had never met Lewis Selby, but in her conversations with her parent had gleaned enough to know that the man seven years her mother's senior sounded a very nice and kind man. He must be nice or her mother would never have allowed him over the doorstep.

'What did you tell him?' she asked, believing her mother needed to talk her present agitated feelings out of her system. She looked at her parent and thought, as she always had, how beautiful her mother was. She had raven hair, too, but the trauma of her life with Archer Fairfax had added a wing of pure white to one side.

Her mother was suddenly looking self-conscious, and all at once confessed, 'I feel a bit of a fool now, but he caught me so unawares at the time that I told him that I never went anywhere without my daughter.'

'You didn't!' Romillie gasped. And, when her mother nodded, 'What did he say to that?' she asked.

'He didn't bat an eye, but straight away suggested that he take the two of us to dinner.'

Heavens! He sounded keen! 'So where are we going?' Romillie teased gently, knowing in advance that her parent had put the kibosh on that notion.

'We aren't. I told Lewis I wouldn't hear of it,' Eleanor replied, as Romillie knew she would. 'I feel dreadful now. I didn't even make him a cup of tea. He just—sort of left.'

All went quiet on the Lewis Selby front after that. Her mother seemed to spend long moments staring into space— though pensively, and not as she had formerly, when her whole world seemed to have imploded.

But a week later Romillie arrived home from work to discover that Lewis had popped in again *and* had been given a cup of tea. In return he had left her mother with a couple of complimentary tickets he could not use himself and which he thought, since it was for an exhibition of paintings at the opening of an art gallery in London on Friday evening, she might be interested in.

'Wasn't that thoughtful?' Eleanor said, more back to the way she had been prior to Lewis's dinner invitation. 'We won't be able to use them, of course, but it was very kind of Lewis to think of us.'

'Why won't we be able to use them?' Romillie asked, not missing that her mother had seemed a touch animated when speaking of the exhibition of paintings.

'Do you think we could—should?' Eleanor asked hesitantly.

'I don't see why not. It would be a shame to waste the tickets if Mr Selby can't use then. And we can easily drive up there when I finish work.'

Eleanor was thoughtful for a minute or so. But suddenly agreed, 'We'll have a cooked meal at lunchtime,' she said. 'Then we'll only need a sandwich before we go.'

Romillie hurried home after on Friday and noticed that her mother was dressed in a pale blue suit, making her look as smart as a new coat of paint. It pleased her—her mother was usually dressed in trousers and an overblouse.

'I can't remember the last time I was in London,' she commented when Romillie, having quickly showered and changed into a smart two-piece, too, headed the car down the drive.

It was ages since her mother had been anywhere, for that matter, and Romillie could only hope she was not too churned up. She would keep an eye on her anyway, and if she looked to be feeling stressed in any way she would get her out of there.

Romillie found that she need not have worried. 'Eleanor! Eleanor Mannion!' someone greeted her the moment they walked into the gallery. She had always painted under her maiden name. And, for all she had not picked up a paintbrush or sold any of her work in years, as several other arty types came up and beamed at her, it was a name that had not been forgotten.

The next half-hour passed quickly as they paused to look, paused to study, prior to moving on. Romillie did not know when she had last seen her mother so animated.

There were a good many people there whom Eleanor did not know, but a good few whom she did. More people came over and expressed warmth and delight at seeing her there so unexpectedly, and Romillie stood back. This was her mother's world, or used to be. And she looked so cheered Romillie could only be glad that they had come.

Then it was just the two of them again, but as her mother turned to point out the merits of one particular picture, Romillie saw her glance to someone else who was making his way over to them. He was a man of average height, smartly suited, and had white hair and looked to be approaching sixty.

'Lewis!' Eleanor exclaimed, a hint of pink creeping up under her skin—and Romillie knew then that there was something more serious going on here than her parent was willing to acknowledge.

'Eleanor! I'm so glad you could make it!'

'I've used your tickets!' she exclaimed apologetically.

'When I knew I would be able to make it after all, I was easily able to get another,' he said with a smile. And, turning to Romillie, 'You must be Eleanor's daughter.'

Romillie studied him for a moment before deciding that she liked the look of him. She had a feeling he would not deliberately harm her mother—and held out her hand. 'Glad to know you, Mr Selby,' she said, for he could be none other.

'Lewis, please,' he suggested, and they shook hands.

And while he and her mother discussed the picture in front of them, and commented on other works to be seen, Romillie for the moment kept to the sidelines while she wondered—had Lewis Selby really been unable to use the tickets he had given her mother? Or, in the face of her refusing to go out with him, had he intended to be there all along, this merely a ploy to have some time with her away from her home? At any rate, he was not moving on, but appeared to have latched on to them.

She was still pondering that matter when she noticed a tall man who must have just come in, because she had not spotted him previously. What especially caught her notice was that the tall, good-looking man, somewhere in his mid-thirties, was standing stock still and just staring at her.

Romillie tilted her chin a trifle—and looked through him. She had seen tall, good-looking men before—tall, good-looking and untrustworthy. She turned back to tune in to what Lewis Selby and her mother were saying. But suddenly they were interrupted when the good-looking man she had been ready to ignore was there, proving that he was not so easy to ignore.

'Naylor!' Lewis exclaimed. 'I thought you were still at the office!'

'I'm taking time off for good behaviour,' Naylor replied, his voice even and well modulated.

'Let me introduce you,' Lewis said pleasantly. 'Naylor is my deputy and will take over when I retire. Naylor, Mrs Eleanor Fairfax.' And, as they shook hands, 'And this is Romillie, Eleanor's daughter.'

'Romillie,' Naylor acknowledged, and shook her hand too, but did not, she thought, seem overly impressed, because he turned from her and straight away asked her mother if she was enjoying the exhibits, and if she had far to come or lived in London.

And while Eleanor explained briefly where they lived, and that they had journeyed up by car, Romillie realised she must have gained the wrong impression when she had thought Naylor Cardell had been standing stock still when he had seen her. If he had, he must have seen all he wanted to, because he was not looking at her now—and in fact had barely given her another glance.

She felt slightly miffed for no reason, because she was sure she did not want the next chairman of Tritel Incorporated to be interested in her—which clearly he was not. So, after first checking that her mother appeared to be all right and in no way anxious, Romillie moved a step or two away to look at a different painting.

From the corner of her eye she saw her mother and Lewis Selby move on. She had thought Naylor Cardell had moved on with them. But—wrong—he was all at once there in front of her.

Romillie looked up and observed that he had short dark blondish hair and quite striking blue eyes—eyes that were looking no more interested now than they had. And—more— were definitely unfriendly. Abruptly, she glanced from him to see that her mother, although now out of earshot, was other- wise chatting happily to Lewis.

Romillie flicked her glance back to Naylor Cardell. She had a feeling she did not like him. Had a feeling he did not like her. Fine. She did not have to like him—if he was standing there waiting for her to say something he'd have a long wait.

But he wasn't waiting. His tone curt, 'You know that Lewis has asked your mother out?' he gritted.

Romillie was so taken aback she wasn't sure that her jaw did not drop. She took another glance to where her mother and Lewis appeared to be getting on famously.

'He told you?' she questioned sharply, not at all sure how she felt about that, but her protective instincts on the upsurge.

'We're friends as well as colleagues,' Naylor Cardell stated. 'Lewis Selby is a fine man,' he went curtly. 'I admire him tremendously.'

Romillie did not care to be spoken to curtly. Who the blazes did he think he was? 'You're suggesting I should join his fan club?' she asked acidly.

Naylor's eyes narrowed at her impudence—Romillie had a feeling that he was more used to women falling at his feet than giving him a load of lip. He swallowed down his ire, however, to inform her, 'Lewis is an honourable man. I can guarantee that should Eleanor take up his invitation she will come to no harm.'

Romillie had had enough of this before it started. He had known her mother for five minutes—she had spent this last five years trying to help her through what had been a very dreadful time for her.

'I'll bear that in mind!' she retorted, and went to walk away—the nerve of the man!

'Hear me out.' Naylor insisted.

Romillie could think of not one single, solitary reason why she should. But, glancing at her mother again, she saw her laugh at something Lewis had just said. And just then she was struck by the change in her mother since that day she had first invited Lewis Selby in for a cup of tea. She seemed, in fact, from that day onwards, to have made great strides in surfacing from the despair that had held her in its grip for so long, and moving on towards regaining her full confidence. So maybe, just maybe, she owed this man—who clearly held Lewis Selby in high regard—some small hearing.

'So?' she invited.

'So I'll tell you,' Naylor Cardell took up, without waiting for her to change her mind, 'because it's for certain that Lewis won't. He went through one horrendous divorce a couple of years ago, where he was too much of a gentleman to fight back. She, the ex, did everything she could to destroy him. She almost succeeded.'

That had such a familiar ring to it—had not her own father tried to undermine her mother at every turn, done everything he could to make her crumple?

'She hated it like hell when he proved too much of a man for her,' Naylor went on. 'But that doesn't mean he didn't suffer just the same.'

Romillie could feel herself warming to Lewis Selby. Oh, the poor man. If… She checked the thought. She mustn't go soft here. Her mother was still her prime consideration.

'So?' she tossed at him, chin jutting.

Naylor Cardell's eyes glinted steel. 'So,' he said heavily, 'from the little Lewis has told me of your mother—and I swear to you he has not broken any confidences,' he added, when she started to bridle, 'I'd say that both your mother and Lewis could do with a break.'

'A break for what?' Romillie questioned hostilely, as ever her mother's guardian.

'A break to get to know each other, wouldn't you say?'

Romillie was not sure that she would. She looked into those striking blue eyes and could feel herself giving in while not sure what she was giving in to. Time to toughen up! 'Who elected you cupid?' she challenged curtly—and discovered that he didn't like being spoken to that way either.

'Look here, Fairfax,' he rapped. 'It's an initial dinner that's in the offing, not a trip to see the vicar. And if you could forget to be thoroughly selfish for two minutes, and after all your mother does for you do something for her for a change, it might improve your disposition.'

Romillie's jaw did drop. That was so unfair! How dared he? She felt like hitting him. But she was used to dampening down her feelings, and so swallowed down the urge to hit him or to tell him just how wrong he had got it. No way was she going to tell him anything of how downcast her mother had been.

So, she stared up at him. Then suddenly she smiled, the phoney smile she had up to then reserved for Jeff Davidson, and with no intention whatsoever of doing anything Naylor Cardell might suggest, 'What would you like me to do?' she invited sweetly.

Whether he saw straight through her or not, Romillie had no idea, but Naylor Cardell seemed to be giving the matter every consideration before, after several moments, he suggested, 'Why not urge Eleanor to take up his dinner invitation? To accept—'

'She won't.' Romillie cut him off. Oh, my, he wasn't used to being interrupted. That was plain as she weathered the exasperated look he sent her.

'Lewis tells me there's a chance if you go too,' he grated.

Oh, help us, this Naylor Cardell really did dislike her, didn't he? She should worry! 'My mother would never agree to that,' Romillie told him forthrightly. But then, out of positively nowhere—though perhaps since he had been trying to back her into a corner where she, it seemed, was selfish and uncaring—Romillie thought it about time she challenged him for a change. 'My mother wouldn't agree to that,' she reiterated, but added, bringing out her phoney smile again, and looking up at him all wide-eyed and innocent, 'But she might agree if we went out in a foursome.'

Naylor Cardell stared at her as if he just could not believe his hearing. As if his normal powers of rapid comprehension had just deserted him.

'Foursome?' he queried slowly. 'We?' he questioned, scandalised.

Suddenly Romillie was having a lovely time. It was all right, wasn't it, when he was doing the challenging, he urging she persuade her mother to accept Lewis's invitation, but different again when that challenge was bounced back at him. 'It's time to put your money where your mouth is,' she told him. And just had to release a light laugh that bubbled up and would not stay down when she added, 'Be brave, Cardell—you've been elected.'

He stared down into her wide brown eyes, looked down at her laughing lovely mouth, and appeared to be very much taken aback—even a little stunned. She was still smiling, not a phoney smile this time, but a genuine smile that came from the fact that in putting him on the spot for a change her good humour was restored. It was not, however, to last.

Because suddenly her own previous phoney smile was being lobbed back at her, and she just did not believe it when, 'Very well,' Naylor Cardell conceded. And, while that wiped the smile from her face, 'I'll make up a foursome,' he agreed, bestowing on her a superior kind of look that had soon put paid to her smile. And, in case she was in any doubt, 'But if your mother still says no,' he added, 'it's off.'

The nerve of the man! Open-mouthed, she stared at him. 'Don't flatter yourself!' she retorted heatedly, having no need of the reminder that he had no personal interest in her but, when he would not normally dream of going out with her, would if it would help out a friend and colleague who had been through very bad times. 'You're not married?' she thought to question, committed, by the look of it, but already searching for a way out.

The trouble was, he seemed to know exactly what she was thinking. It was all there in his silkily drawled, 'You don't get out of it that easily. I'm completely unattached—and like it that way.'

Romillie breathed out heavily. 'Good for you!' she erupted, niggled, and was more annoyed when he took out his business card and handed it to her.

'Call me,' he said.

She did not want his wretched card, but without another word took it from him. Fuming, she turned from him and went in search of her mother. 'You don't get out of it that easily' he had said. She did not like the sound of that. Somehow, those words had sounded ominously like a threat!

# CHAPTER TWO

ROMILLIE awoke early on Saturday morning, hardly able to believe the happenings of the previous evening. Naylor Cardell had thought her selfish and with little thought for anyone but herself. As if she cared what he thought! And he expected her to give him a call! He'd had that! She had no intention of ringing him *ever*!

She had not seen him again after she had walked away, so presumably he had viewed all he wanted in the art gallery. When she and her mother had been ready to leave Lewis Selby had enquired if they would care to join him somewhere for a bite of supper. Romillie had waited for her mother to reply, but hadn't been surprised when she declined the invitation.

'I think we'll be on our way.'

'You've enjoyed the evening?' Lewis had asked, escorting them to where they had parked the car.

'Much more than I thought I would,' Eleanor had replied, and had given him such a sweet smile.

Romillie and her mother had discussed various paintings on the way home. But Romillie had been hard put to know how to reply when her mother got round to mentioning some of the people they had met, in particular one Naylor Cardell.

'What did you think of him?' she had asked.

Arrogant, curt, bossy, wanted taking down a peg or five, sprang to mind. 'I should imagine he'll make a very good suc-

cessor to Lewis,' was what she did say, which in fairness—
given that she knew little about the business—she thought he
probably would.

'You seemed to be getting on well with him,' Eleanor commented. 'I glanced over to you a couple of times and you
seemed to be chatting well away there—he was making you
smile and laugh a lot, I noticed.'

Somehow, with her mother having had such a happy
evening, it had not seemed fair to put a blight on it by confess-
ing that, while her laugh had been genuine, her smiles—as
well as his—had been bogus.

It warmed her though, that while she had kept her eye on
her mother from time to time, to check she was coping all right
on her first outing in a long, long while, her mother, it seemed,
had likewise been keeping a motherly and protective eye on
her daughter.

Over the next few days Romillie was able to observe that
there was a growing dramatic change in her parent of late. She
was generally much, much brighter than she had been. And on
Wednesday when Romillie went in from work, she actually
heard her singing as she pottered about the kitchen.

The reason for that, Romillie began to see, was because
Lewis Selby had called that afternoon. 'Is that an extra cup and
saucer I see?' Romillie asked lightly of the two cups and saucers
on the draining board.

'Lewis popped in,' her mother replied.

Romillie had done nothing about phoning Naylor Cardell,
but all at once she began to wonder if she should. She had an
idea that Lewis Selby was in no hurry to complete closing up
the house next door and putting it on the market. But his
business there must surely finish soon.

From her own observations she had seen how knowing
Lewis had done her mother nothing but good. Since knowing
him she had come on in leaps and bounds.

She guessed he had an understanding of her mother that only someone who had been through the pulverising divorce he had been through could have. Instinctively Romillie knew that he would guard her mother. Which made her wonder how her mother would feel when Lewis did not come around any more.

But—Naylor Cardell…? Oh, for crying out loud, it was only dinner, for goodness' sake! But *he* would be there too—now, that was the maggot in the apple.

Frustratedly, irritatedly, she chewed over having to meet the wretched man again. Could she, in the interests of getting her parent into the swing of socialising again, put up with him for a few hours?

With a heartfelt sigh Romillie reluctantly came to the conclusion that in an attempt to wean her mother away from her reclusive existence—whether Lewis Selby featured in her future or not—she had better make that phone call.

Though first she had to get her mother to agree to the foursome—it just did not bear thinking about, Romillie considered, that she should dine *à deux*, just her and Naylor Cardell there. Though from what she could remember of his obvious dislike of her that was never going to happen anyway.

She was still seeking a way to broach the subject when they were having their meal that night and she became aware that her mother was looking solemnly at her. 'Have I gravy on my chin?' Romillie asked puzzled.

'You're not—man-wary, are you, darling?' Eleanor questioned in a rush.

'No, of course not.' Romillie protested.

But could see she was not believed when her mother pressed on worriedly, 'You haven't let the way your father is, the way he behaved in our marriage, put you off men in any way?' she persisted.

If it had, and while she might privately be concerned in case she developed some of her father's lax traits, there was no way

Romillie was going to give her mother something else to worry about.

'What brought this on?' she asked with a laugh.

'You,' Eleanor replied, not laughing. 'You never go out with a man more than a few times. And just when I was beginning to think you were going steady with Jeff Davidson you broke up with him.'

'I'm perfectly happy as I am!' Romillie protested.

But Eleanor was suddenly far more determined than she had been for a very long while. 'I know you've had to spend a lot of time with me, and I regret that more than you know. But I'm okay again now, and I want to stand on my own feet. So I want you to promise me that instead of being negative the next time some agreeable man asks you out, you'll say yes.'

This was quite a speech from her mother. 'If it will stop you worrying—yes, yes, yes,' Romillie cheerfully agreed, happily aware that she never went anywhere where she might meet one such.

'Good,' her mother responded. 'Lewis told me this afternoon that Naylor Cardell had mentioned having dinner with you.'

'That's unfair!' Romillie cried, trying to look outraged, but delighted to see a sudden gleam of wickedness in her mother's eyes. Agreeable? Naylor Cardell!

'You've just promised.' She refused to let her back down.

And at that moment Romillie knew she had the opening she had been looking for—forget the 'agreeable' bit. But she tried to keep it very casual as she brought out, 'I will if you will.'

'I'm not with you?'

'Lewis Selby asked you to have dinner with him,' Romillie reminded her.

'Oh, I couldn't,' her mother straight away exclaimed.

'You could if we went in a foursome.'

Eleanor looked at her in amazement. 'A foursome!' She thought about it, and then decided, 'You don't want me with you. And what on earth would Naylor say?'

Romillie already had the answer to that—either your mother comes or I don't. 'That's the deal,' she said, and refused to budge.

'But that will mean asking Lewis,' she protested.

'I'll get Naylor to ask him.'

'How did this all get so complicated?' her mother prevaricated.

'It's not complicated. Lewis and Naylor, you and me, or nothing.'

'But Lewis hasn't asked me out again,' Eleanor stated. Though, as if the idea was starting to sound not quite so unthinkable as it had, she suddenly looked as though she quite liked the idea. Even if she did insist, 'I'll come, but only if Lewis rings and asks me.' With that she began to clear their dinner plates seeming a shade foxed all at once as she commented, 'All I thought to do was to find out if you have a hang up about men—and suddenly it looks as if I'm to get my best dress out of mothballs.'

Romillie did not look forward to making that phone call, and got up the next morning with the fact that she was going to have to hanging over her like a dark cloud. But, since she did not want to make the call from her workstation, she went out to her car mid-morning and from there rang the number on Naylor Cardell's business card.

'May I speak with Mr Cardell?' she asked the female who answered, and realised that the number gave her access straight through to his PA. She half hoped the PA would block the call or say he was not in.

But no such luck. 'Who shall I say is calling?' she enquired pleasantly.

'Romillie Fairfax,' she replied, and waited, wanting to terminate the call before she started.

'Yes?' clipped Naylor Cardell, not very enamoured to have his work interrupted.

'We can make Saturday,' she told him briefly, her tones not enamoured of him either.

'Right,' he said, and that was all.

But, fearing he was about to bang down his phone, Romillie hurriedly burst into speech. 'But my mother will only agree if Lewis contacts her and asks her personally.'

'I'll see to it!' Naylor clipped, without so much as a pause—and that was an end to the time he wasted on her.

That urge she had felt before, to set about him, was there again. She did not know what it was about him but Romillie experienced a quite dreadful desire to punch Naylor Cardell's head. She half wished he had changed his mind and said that he wasn't free on Saturday, and that dinner was off.

But, on leaving her car and going back to work, Romillie realised that to wish that would only make her as selfish as the dratted man thought she was. Not that she was concerned about his opinion. It was her mother that mattered.

But Naylor Cardell had 'seen to it', as he had said he would, and when Romillie went home at lunchtime it was to discover that Lewis had already been in telephone contact with her mother.

'I said we would meet them in town to save them driving down here, but Lewis wouldn't hear of it,' Eleanor revealed. 'He and Naylor will pick us up around seven—but I expect you already know that from Naylor.'

By half past six on Saturday evening, Romillie was starting to have grave doubts about the venture. Her mother was looking more and more uptight by the minute.

Which only went to make Romillie wonder if she should have left things well alone and let her mother come to a decision in her own time about whether or not she wanted to go out in male company.

At five to seven, with her parent growing more and more fidgety, Romillie was feeling very much that she had been wrong to collude with Naylor Cardell the way that she had. In fact, she was of a mind to go out and apologise to Lewis—and

Naylor if she had to—and to tell them they would not be coming to dine with them after all.

Impossibly, however, when her mother had been pacing about for the last ten minutes, no sooner had Lewis arrived and said a quiet, 'Hello, Eleanor,' than her mother's nerves about the evening seem to instantly fall away.

Looking completely relaxed with each other, they were already engaged in pleasantries when Naylor unfolded his long length from behind the steering wheel of the car and came to join them.

'Romillie,' he said.

'Naylor,' she replied.

And that would have been it as far as she was concerned—except that both her mother and Lewis seemed to be of the opinion that Naylor was her date, and insisted that she sit up front with him.

'Had a good week?' she enquired, after racking her brains for something to talk to him about as they drove along.

'Can't complain,' he replied briefly. A minute ticked by, and then two. 'You?' he enquired.

Grief, this was like trying to harvest a field of wheat with a pair of blunt scissors! 'Average,' she managed, and began to be sure that the evening was going to be a complete disaster.

Strangely, it wasn't. Not totally. Whoever had chosen the restaurant Naylor and Lewis took them to they had, Romillie saw, chosen well. There was plush carpeting, crisp linen, and room between the well-spaced tables for private conversation. If, that was, they could find anything to talk about.

But she had to give Naylor Cardell credit that, the idea of the four of them dining together being hers and not his, he did not leave it to her to keep the conversational ball rolling. As they started on their meal, he did away with desultory conversation and appeared to show an interest in her. She knew that it was purely for her mother's benefit, but felt the oddest sensation inside when he looked across at her for long moments and seemed quite taken with her. She saw his glance flick over her just below shoulder-length long dark hair, stray over her un-blemished complexion, before his striking blue eyes connected with her velvety brown ones.

'Eleanor, I know, is a well-known artist of exceptional talent,' he began engagingly. 'Tell me, Romillie, have you in-herited your mother's gift?'

'Er—I've tried, but I'm quite, quite hopeless,' she stated honestly, endeavouring to hide the fact that his charm offensive had taken her unawares.

'Oh, I wouldn't say that, darling.' Her mother joined in the conversation, amazingly, after the way she had been prior to seeing Lewis that evening, now thoroughly relaxed.

'I think you must be seeing my poor efforts through a mother's indulgent eyes,' Romillie laughed, and, feeling unex-pectedly relaxed herself all at once, fell silent for a while as Lewis joined in and the discussion centred around art, includ-ing talk of the exhibition all four of them had attended.

They were on to the next course when there was a lull in the conversation and Naylor again seemed to remember that, in the interests of furthering the budding friendship of Lewis and Eleanor, he should be showing more of an interest in Eleanor's daughter.

'What sort of work do you do, Romillie?' he asked. 'You never said.'

'I work in a dental practice,' she replied, realising she was honour-bound to play along.

'You're a dental surgeon?'

'Nothing so grand,' she answered, finding a smile. 'I'm just a receptionist.'

'As long as you enjoy it,' he responded, and asked, 'Have you been there long?'

'About a year,' she replied, and realised he was playing his interested man-friend part well when he did not leave it there.

'What did you do before that?' he enquired pleasantly.

Nothing, actually. But for no known reason, while she was sure she was not the smallest bit bothered about his opinion of her, Romillie discovered that—when he must work very hard—she didn't wish that he should add lazy to his belief that she was selfish.

'I—er…' she stumbled—and was astonished that when she had spent the last five years doing what she could to protect her mother, her mother, plainly knowing her well enough to read her discomfiture, suddenly took on the role of *protecting her!*

'Romillie was about to start university in the hope of one day being a forensic scientist, but she gave up her university place to stay at home and—keep me company when I became unwell,' Eleanor butted in.

'Mum…' Romillie murmured. 'You don't have to…'

But Eleanor, her protective instinct dormant for so long, had woken up with a vengeance, clearly not wanting her daughter's 'escort' to think her offspring had spent years in total idleness. 'I was—very—down, and would have been lost without Rom,' she went on to explain.

Romillie had never heard her mother talk like this, and, aware that Naylor's glance had switched from her mother and on to her, started to feel a little embarrassed. 'Mum, please,' she protested.

'It's true, darling,' Eleanor said affectionately. 'You've had to be strong for both of us.'

Thankfully Lewis entered the conversation just then, to gently enquire, 'How are you progressing now, Eleanor?'

'Getting there,' she replied, favouring him with a warm smile. 'With my daughter's help, I'm getting there. Romillie has taken this job well below her capabilities because it's near enough to home that she can return in her lunch hour—or be with me inside fifteen minutes if I start to get a little bit panicky.'

Romillie by that time was feeling dreadfully torn—as well

as embarrassed. On the one hand it was so good to hear her mother—if a little hesitantly—opening up. But on the other, re-calling how only last Wednesday her parent had wondered if she had been put off men, Romillie could not help but think was she now trying to show Naylor, lest Romillie show him her 'negative' side, that her daughter really did have a caring, positive side. Oh, grief!

But she did not believe for a moment that Naylor was aware of her embarrassment, or was endeavouring to take the atten-tion off her when, quite pleasantly he glanced over to her mother and enquired, 'And how about your own work, Eleanor?'

'I hadn't picked up my brushes in I don't know how long, but I've recently done a few small pieces, nothing major,' she responded, and Romillie drew a relieved breath to have the limelight taken off her. 'But I do believe I'm getting the itch to get back to it again,' her mother, to Romillie's delight, stated.

'You wouldn't like to make a portrait of me your first as-signment, I suppose?' Lewis asked. And, when Eleanor turned to him as if ready to refuse, 'Mind, you'd have to make me look good,' he added, and laughed with Eleanor when she laughed. And Lewis explained, 'Apparently all past chairmen have to be hanged in the boardroom. Many say not before time,' he joked.

All in all, given that she had been overwhelmingly embar-rassed by her mother singing her praises, Romillie thought the evening had been most successful. Her mother had smiled and laughed with Lewis, and in fact, as Romillie sat beside Naylor Cardell on the journey home, she could not remember the last time she had seen her mother so buoyant.

Naylor pulled his car up on the drive of her home, and out of courtesy both men got out of the car. The evening, in Romillie's view, should have ended there. So she did not thank Naylor Cardell when he chose to extend it. Though it was plain that his interest was not in her—not that she wanted it to be, for heaven's sake—because it was to her mother that he addressed his question.

'I wonder, Eleanor,' he said as the four of them stood on the drive, 'if you would be kind enough to show me some of your work?'

She looked about to politely turn down the request. Then she looked from him to her daughter, and Romillie had to endure that feeling of embarrassment again. For it seemed to her that while it might appear obvious to anyone else that since—if she accepted—her mother had been commissioned to paint a portrait of his company's chairman, it was likely someone on the board would want to see something of her work, Romillie saw it differently. From her mother's point of view one very agreeable man was taking an interest in her man-wary daughter. It was time for a mother to wake up and do something about it. In this small case—since Naylor obviously wanted to prolong the evening—agree.

'I haven't got very much I can show you in the way of work I used to do, but there are a few paintings scattered about in my studio—as well as several I didn't want to sell. Come in,' she invited. 'My studio's on the south-west facing side of the house.'

As they went along the hall, pausing to study one rather lovely landscape Eleanor had painted many years previously, Romillie, very much needing to be on her own, decided she was not needed on this part of the tour.

'I'll make some coffee,' she mumbled to anyone interested to hear, and headed for the kitchen.

Had she hoped to have some peace from this situation that was more or less of her own making, she soon discovered it was not to be. She had not so much as lifted down the coffee jar when she heard a sound nearby, and turned her head to find that Naylor Cardell had joined her.

'Want any help?' he enquired, his good-looking face giving away nothing of what he was thinking or feeling.

Romillie shook her head. 'No thanks.' She turned to face

him, and releasing a pent-up breath, 'We should never have done it,' she stated flatly.

'Oh, come on!' Naylor argued. Though he conceded, 'We probably wouldn't have, had I not provoked you by calling you selfish. And for that I do apologise—'

'Oh, grief, don't!' Romillie butted in to protest, remembering again the way her mother had been singing her praises. 'I know we meant well by trying to get my mother and Lewis to get to know each other more outside the home—' that, after all, had been what this 'foursome' had been about '—but now my mother thinks you and I are—um—interested in each other.'

'A natural assumption, surely?'

'She probably thinks you've sloped away specifically to see me.'

'Given that our aim is to have Lewis and Eleanor break down a few walls, is that such a bad impression to give?' he enquired urbanely.

Romillie sighed. 'It will be when I don't see you again.'

'Sorry to be obtuse,' Naylor commented, seeming to fill their not so small kitchen, 'but I can't see what you're getting at.'

She thought him anything but obtuse. Indeed, to be in the position he was at Tritel Incorporated in his mid-thirties, showed he must be as sharp as a tack.

Then she suddenly saw something else. 'You knew I was embarrassed, didn't you? At dinner, when my mother was busy setting you right about my selfish streak?'

'It occurred to me you weren't feeling too comfortable,' he admitted.

Romillie stared at him. Somehow she had never thought of him as sensitive. But he had to be to have picked up how she was feeling. Not only that, but in that sensitivity he had taken the conversation away from her and given her chance to recover by asking her mother about her work.

'You're nicer than I first thought,' Romillie admitted slowly.

'Steady,' he warned. Theirs was not the sort of relationship where either had been complimentary to the other. But then he smiled, a most wonderful smile, and all of a sudden Romillie's heart seemed to quicken up its beat.

It was a totally new experience for her, and she looked away from him, feeling oddly tongue-tied. 'I know my mother was only thinking of me,' she said hurriedly when she found her voice. 'But that's purely because—' Romillie came to an abrupt halt. Good heavens, Naylor Cardell might have shown himself to be nicer than she had thought, but there was no need to go overboard and tell him...

'Because?' Naylor pressed when she did not go on.

'Nothing,' she said. And then realised that the next chairman of Tritel Incorporated did not believe in 'nothing' answers.

'So tell me,' he insisted.

'I'd better make a start on this coffee.'

'Eleanor was only thinking of you when she was telling me how special you are because...?'

Romillie looked at him, unsmiling. To hold out any longer seemed to her to be making a far bigger issue of it than it was. And anyway, she would not be seeing him again. Just another half an hour or so more of his company and that would be it.

'My mother seems to think I'm a bit anti-men,' she said in a rush.

His lips twitched. 'It shows,' he drawled, and she knew he was thinking of their first unfriendly encounter.

'Oh, shut up!' she exclaimed, but her lips twitched too.

'Don't leave it there,' he commanded.

'You're confusing me!'

'Your mother thinks you're anti-men, so she impressed on me how lovely you are because...'

'I'm getting embarrassed again,' Romillie erupted. But

probably because of that, suddenly wanting it all said, she went rushing on, 'I don't know—perhaps she believes you are the new man in my life—'

'What happened to the old one?' he cut in, in her opinion too sharp by half.

She went on as if he had not spoken. 'My mother wants you to know more about the real me before the hang-up she worries I might have about men kicks in, and...'

'You have a hang-up about men?' Naylor queried, those striking blue eyes holding her fast, his expression serious.

'I don't think so.'

'You're—how old?'

'What's that got to do with anything?' she wanted to know.

'Ever been engaged?'

'Grief—I'm not interested in marriage!' she exclaimed indignantly. Hadn't she seen enough of marriage in this very house to know she would rather die an old maid than take the marriage route?

'Your parents are divorced, I believe?' he queried.

But if he had any more questions lined up—tough.

'Sorry, Naylor. Would you mind if I got up from the analyst's couch?' And, not waiting for an answer, 'It was no problem for me to tell you what I have, because I know that after tonight I'm never going to see you again. But that's it! One "date" does not entitle you to an in-depth personal history.'

'And your mother wonders what it is about you that so puts men off, so she decided to let your "latest beau" know how lovely you really are?'

Latest beau! She'd like to bury a hatchet in his head! Romillie's dislike of him was back in full force. 'I've never been dumped yet!' she flared hostilely.

'That's usually your prerogative?'

'Clear off, Cardell!' she fumed.

Naylor looked back at her, those keen blue eyes taking in

her hostility. Then, giving her a hard, thoughtful stare, 'Black, no sugar,' he ordered, and left her.

Romillie set about making coffee, never more glad that he had gone. He could find his own way to the studio; she'd had it with him.

She had expected them back well before the coffee was ready, but when they were not she went in search of them. Perhaps her mother meant her to take a tray into the studio? She hadn't thought so, but…

Romillie entered the studio, thinking she could easily collect a tray, but was immediately struck by the fact that, while Naylor was up one end of the studio, her mother and Lewis were down at the other. And, what was more, they were standing close, and were so engrossed in the picture they were studying, and looked so much 'a couple' somehow, that it just did not seem right to break in.

She took a few silent steps nearer to the man she was now certain she had no liking for and noticed he had been looking at her mother's more recent work, in particular a painting of one section of the rear garden.

Then suddenly, as Naylor put that picture down and picked up another, so Romillie recalled what other recent pictures were up that end. In a rush, she went quickly to him. But she was already too late!

She'd opened her mouth to protest when, reaching Naylor, she saw him standing gazing fascinated at the nude sketch her mother had made of her. It was a three-quarter side-on sketch, showing the lovely curve of her back as she bent slightly over, her behind, and the long length of leg from hip, thigh, calf and toe. The sketch showed her tiny waist and moved up to the full globe of her right breast and part of her left breast. Above her unadorned shoulder and the long length of neck her mother had captured in her face a most becoming honest and true smile, a smile that seemed to shine out through her eyes too.

'That picture's not for sale!' Romillie found her voice to tell him huskily, while at the same time wanting to snatch it from his hands.

Naylor studied the sketch for a moment to two longer, taking in the complete beauty Eleanor Mannion-Fairfax had captured. Unhurriedly, then he turned to Romillie. If he had observed that her cheeks had a hint of warm pink about them he gave no sign, but, his eyes telling her nothing, 'Strangely enough,' he drawled, 'I wasn't thinking of buying.'

How she kept civil to him after that, Romillie never knew. But as Naylor put the picture down, and Eleanor and Lewis suddenly seemed to notice they had company and came over, Romillie somehow retained enough good manners to not let anyone else feel uncomfortable.

But she was glad to see Naylor go. As anticipated, he did not ask to see her again. She would have been astonished—and pleased to turn him down—had he done so.

But the man disturbed her. She acknowledged that. He was in her head again when she awoke on Sunday morning. She half regretted that she had suggested the foursome at all. But then, recalling the way her mother and Lewis were with each other, nothing showy, but quiet and sort of—together, she could only know that at whatever cost to her personally it had been the right thing to do.

Not that she could say it had cost her that much. Just more intimate than she would have wanted *tête-à-tête* in the kitchen with Naylor Cardell, that was all. They had soon established that they weren't going to see each other again—and he was as pleased about that as she was.

It was a mystery to her why Naylor should still be in her head when she went into work on Monday. She ousted him when the first person she saw was Jeff Davidson. 'You're still coming with me to Alex Yardley's retirement dinner on Saturday, I hope?' he asked, laying on the charm.

Romillie had in part forgotten that Friday would be Mr Yardley's last day in the practice, and had forgotten totally that, although the invitation was for 'and guest', she and Jeff had been going to go together.

'Sorry,' she apologised. And, knowing it would be discourteous not to attend, 'I'm bringing someone else.'

He did not like that. 'The new boyfriend, I suppose?' he questioned, not very pleasantly.

Actually, she had been thinking of asking her mother if she would like to come. 'If he's free,' she replied.

'If he's free?' Jeff queried, and with a calculating look in his eyes, 'There isn't anybody else, is there? You've made him up!' he accused.

'He seemed real enough to me over the weekend,' she replied, and had Naylor back in her head again. She had to smile to herself, though—he'd be delighted to know he was her new boyfriend.

Romillie asked her mother how she felt about going to the dinner on Saturday. But as she had expected, although Eleanor had made a start on socialising again, she was not keen on mixing with a load of strangers whom she had never met before.

'Why not ask Naylor?' she suggested. 'I'm sure he'd be only too pleased to be your date.'

Oh, heavens. Romillie did so hope her mother was not worrying that she had such a 'thing' about men that she was going to push her in the male direction at every chance.

'I'll give it some thought,' she replied, a little fib permissible in the circumstances, she felt. 'Talking of thoughts, have you thought any more about painting Lewis's portrait?'

Eleanor smiled at her, and confessed, 'I have to say I have.'

'And?'

'Oh, I don't know, Rom. I'm pulled to do it a lot of the time. Sometimes I feel really keen to have a shot at it. But at others I feel sure I'll make a complete hash of it.'

It was plain from that that her mother's former confidence in her ability had not fully returned. 'How about accepting the commission on the basis that if you mess it up, or Lewis does not like it, you reserve the right not to sell it to him?'

Eleanor considered the idea. 'But what about the time he'll waste coming here? I shall need at least two or three sittings!'

Romillie had to smile. 'Mother, dear,' she teased gently, 'I've an idea Lewis won't consider it time wasted whether there's a portrait for him to hang in the boardroom at the end of it or not.'

Her mother went a delicate shade of pink. 'Oh, you,' she said, but did allow herself a quiet smile.

Romillie had supposed her mother would discuss the portrait with Lewis when he came down again, but when on Thursday evening he had not been down to Tarnleigh at all, her mother revealed that he'd got a lot going on in his office that week.

'I wonder,' Eleanor began, stopped, and then started off again. 'Do you fancy acting as my agent, Rom?'

Romillie had no idea what an artist's agent did, but, 'What would you like me to do?' she asked.

'Would you like to get in touch with Lewis and—um—arrange for his first sitting? That is,' she added hurriedly, 'if he still wants me to do it.'

By the sound of it, her mother was nervous of broaching the subject to Lewis, and, aware as Romillie was of her mother's quite exceptional ability at her artist's easel, she could feel herself getting quite uptight. She knew they had Archer Fairfax to thank that her mother's confidence had been so badly fractured.

Talk at the surgery the next morning was all about the retirement dinner the following evening. Jeff Davidson, clearly not believing she had found anyone to replace him in her life, had halted her to quiz her every day since Monday as to whom she was bringing as her guest. But it was not until Brenda, Mr Yardley's dental nurse, who was organising the event, asked her for her guest's name for a place card that Romillie realised she had been a bit tardy.

'I…' was as far as she'd got to saying that a place name would not be necessary, when she suddenly spotted Jeff Davidson hovering. 'I'm not sure yet if he can make it. Can I let you know later, Brenda?'

'No probs,' Brenda said cheerfully, and went to round up the next tardy individual.

'Keeping you dangling, is he?' Jeff Davidson smirked.

It was at that point that Romillie wondered what she had ever seen in Jeff Davidson! But still the same she was human enough to want to bring someone to the dinner, if only to wipe that smirk off his face.

On her parent's behalf, she went out to her car to phone Lewis during her mid-morning break. She did not want to ring Naylor's office number, so rang the main switchboard. Lewis was in a meeting, she discovered, which was a pity. With her mother's confidence much improved but still very rocky, Romillie wanted it all to be a *fait accompli* before her parent should change her mind.

She guessed it would be impossible to contact him at lunchtime, but went out to her car mid-afternoon and tried again. 'Mr Selby isn't in the building just now,' the telephonist reported. 'Can anyone else help?'

'Is Mr Naylor Cardell available?' she asked without thinking, and wondered what on earth had come over her. She didn't want to speak to him, for goodness' sake!

Though, before she could end the call, she heard Naylor's voice enquiring, 'Romillie?'

'Um…' She felt so het-up suddenly she had completely forgotten she had given the telephonist her name when asking for Lewis. 'I—er…' She pulled herself together. 'Actually, I wanted to have a word with Lewis, only he's not around just now.' Silence. 'Um, I wonder…'

'I'll be seeing him later. Would you like me to ask him to give you a call?'

'Er…' Never had she felt so indecisive. 'My mother is willing to paint his portrait, only she's not feeling very confident about it. I wanted to discuss it with him…'

'Don't worry,' Naylor said kindly. 'I'm sure Lewis appreciates how things are. I know he wouldn't dream of upsetting Eleanor.'

'Thank you,' Romillie said quietly, and would have ended the call right there. But apparently, if she had finished, Naylor had not.

'I'm glad to have the chance to have a word,' he said before she had shut down.

'You are?'

'I don't feel I apologised adequately for misjudging you the way I did,' he said charmingly. 'If there's anything I can do to make amends…' he was adding, when she saw Jeff Davidson come out to collect something from his car.

'You're going to regret saying that,' she said on impulse.

'I am?' She didn't think he sounded too worried.

She took a deep breath, and plunged. 'One of the senior partners here is retiring and is giving a retirement dinner tomorrow evening.' She swallowed, but, having got started on this—though heaven alone knew how—she felt obliged to carry on. 'How would you feel about being my guest?'

Dead silence at the other end. She knew then that he wouldn't. Was sure of it when at long last he spoke. 'I thought I'd been dumped,' he drawled.

'You? Never!' she said, totally unable to imagine anyone dumping him—and somehow just had to laugh. But, as her light tinkle of laughter died away, she let him off the hook. 'You don't have to.'

'What time?' he asked.

Romillie found she was smiling when she went back indoors. As soon as she was able she let Brenda know that the name of her guest was Mr Naylor Cardell.

Funnily, as she drove home, and when she had not been looking forward to the dinner all that much, she found that she was feeling quite light-hearted about it.

'Your agent left a message for Lewis,' she told her mother when she went in. 'He wasn't available when I phoned.'

'You left a message with his PA?' Eleanor sound a little discomfited about that.

'Naylor, actually,' Romillie replied.

'You spoke to Naylor?'

'Er—um—I've invited him to Mr Yardley's dinner tomorrow,' Romillie said in a rush. And, at her mother's expression of pleased surprise, 'Now, don't read anything into that. He's just… It's just dinner.'

'Yes, dear. Anything you say, Rom.'

It *was* just dinner, Romillie affirmed to herself as she got ready for Naylor to call the following evening. While she was anxious that her parent should not keep up with this idea that her daughter was 'man-wary', she equally did not want her nursing the idea that she and Naylor were attracted to each other.

Though, when a short while later Romillie opened the door to him, she had to admit that Naylor Cardell was something else again! She even had to take a small gasp of breath when tall, immaculately suited, he stood there and just let his eyes rove over her for a moment.

'Romillie,' he greeted her coolly, when he had finished his inspection of her in a red dress that apart from thin straps left her shoulders bare.

'Naylor,' she replied, feeling breathless all of a sudden. 'Come in.'

She took him into the sitting room so he should say hello to her mother, and while he chatted to her parent, remarking that Lewis was exceptionally pleased that she had consented to paint his portrait and would be in touch, Romillie got herself back together again.

By the time she and Naylor were in his car and on their way to the dinner venue, she had long since scorned the notion that she had been in any way remotely breathless at seeing Naylor again.

Though she could not help noticing as she introduced him to those near that he seemed to have that effect on one or two of her female colleagues.

The evening was going well, she felt, and for a short while it started to be even better when over dinner, with everyone seated at a long table, she caught Jeff Davidson scowling at her. Good! Nobody smirked at her expense. She smiled sweetly at him and turned to Naylor—and promptly forgot whatever comment she had been going to make when she realised that he had been watching her. She realised that he had seen her smiling at the other man. And, from the hard glint that was suddenly in Naylor's fine blue eyes, she got the impression that he did not care very much for her 'making eyes' at someone else while he was her escort.

Oh, crumbs. Not that she had been 'making eyes' at Jeff Davidson, but she supposed in her effort to thumb her nose at him she had looked at him overlong.

Since it appeared that she had just, without a word being said, been brought to task for bad manners, Romillie made a point of concentrating on her escort for the rest of the evening.

Naylor was not impressed. The evening progressed, and the dinner ended with Terence East, now the senior partner, presenting Mr Yardley with a very fine cut-glass bowl, and Mr Yardley giving a short speech. But Romillie was aware the whole time that, while Naylor remained courteous and well-mannered throughout, he was very much annoyed with her.

It did not help matters when, as the evening broke up and everyone made to depart, there was a jam of people by the door and she found she was standing right next to Jeff Davidson.

'Super evening, wasn't it?' she said brightly.

'If you like that sort of thing,' he replied sulkily. 'You seemed to be enjoying yourself anyway.'

'I had a wonderful time,' she replied, and, as Naylor appeared by her side, 'Naylor, I don't think I introduced Jeffrey Davidson—he's one of the dentists I work for. Jeff, my—er—friend, Naylor Cardell.'

She had to give Naylor top marks for sophistication, because while Jeff just stood there looking peeved, 'Davidson,' Naylor acknowledged smoothly, and, space opening up in front of them, took hold of Romillie's upper arm and guided her into it.

Romillie was aware that Naylor had nothing he wanted to say to her as they drove towards her home. Nor could she think of a thing to say to him. Fortunately the journey was not a long one, but she could feel a kind of tension in the car the whole while.

Naylor pulled his car onto the drive and she wondered if he expected her to invite him in for coffee, and whether she should. He had a way to go if he was driving back to London.

'I hope the evening wasn't too tedious for you,' she commented as they stood in the porch by her front door.

Had she expected some polite and pleasant rejoinder, however, she did not get one. Facing her in the light from the porch lamp, 'I don't care to be made use of!' Naylor gritted.

'Made use of?' she protested.

'If you were trying to make your boyfriend jealous—you succeeded!' he bit aggressively.

'Boyfriend?'

'Don't come the innocent with me!' he rapped. 'I'm on to you, Fairfax!'

'I don't know what you mean?'

'Hmmph!' he grunted, to show what he thought of that. 'Davidson might have come down with the last rain shower—I didn't!'

'Davidson—Jeff?'

Naylor did not deign to answer, but his hands snaked out and caught a none too gentle hold of her arms. 'Tell me straight,' he demanded. 'But for Davidson, would you have asked me to be your partner this evening?'

Oh, grief, put like that, Romillie could see that Naylor was right—she *had* used him. 'I'm—sorry,' she apologised.

Only her apology, her confirmation, seemed more to anger him than to appease him. And, as if needing a release from that anger, Naylor abruptly pulled her into his arms. Even as she stood staring up at him, momentarily stunned, his head was coming down.

And, all before she knew it, his well-shaped mouth was over hers and he was kissing her angrily, drawing her body close up to his.

'No!' she protested on a broken whisper.

But her mouth was not free for longer than that one word before his lips claimed hers again. Although this time the heat of anger was fading, and gradually his kiss became gentle, warm and seeking.

Romillie did not want to respond. In fact she could not have said quite when her protest of 'No' became an inviting 'Yes', but all at once, as his kiss gentled out, so sensations new to her began to overtake her.

She wanted to hold him. As he held her close, she wanted to hold him close. She put her arms around him and, as his kiss deepened, so she knew that she—wanted him!

Shaken, and with the knowledge of what he had stirred in her roaring in her head, she somehow managed to push him from her. She had no idea if she was looking as shaken as she felt, but as she stared up at him in shock, so Naylor, looking a touch speechless himself, took a step back, his arms dropping from her.

Though he was the first to find his voice. 'That, Romillie Fairfax,' he said, sounding tough, 'is the least you owe me.' And with that he did a smart about-turn.

As his car sped off down the drive, Romillie came to her

senses and stared after it, horrified. Had that been her a few moments ago? She barely knew the man and yet she had felt... Oh, no, please, please, say that it wasn't!

# CHAPTER THREE

ROMILLIE was awake at first light on Sunday. She had slept badly, and was beset by the same worrying question that had plagued her from the moment last night when Naylor had walked away from her. Had she inherited her father's baser instincts?

It was a terrifying thought, and one that over the years had returned from time to time to torment her. Though it was only last night when she had been in Naylor's arms, when she had felt that urge to—not hold back. So was in any wonder that she had slept badly?

Her mother had been in bed when she had got in, but had called, 'Have a good time, darling?'

Romillie knew she could have gone into her mother's room and chatted the evening over. But for once she had felt a need to be by herself.

She was still fretting about the way she had parted from Naylor when she left her bed, showered, and got dressed. She instantly recalled the feel of his strong arms around her—recalled his second kiss—and her reaction to it. She had so enjoyed the feel of his wonderful mouth over hers that, incredibly, she had been unaware of anything but her need to get closer and yet closer to him.

Feeling very shaken, if not still in shock, at realising the type of person a man of the world like Naylor could make her,

Romillie went downstairs, knowing that whatever else happened that day she was going to have to keep that disturbing self-knowledge from her mother.

Which, in actual fact, turned out to be easier than she had thought, in that her mother smilingly revealed that she'd had a visitor last night. For one dreadful panicky moment Romillie thought her father had called. One visit from him could send her mother straight back into her shell. But her mother wasn't looking pale or tearful, she was smiling.

'Lewis?' Romillie guessed.

'He didn't stay long,' Eleanor confirmed, and over breakfast revealed that he was delighted she had agreed to paint his portrait. 'I shall need some fresh art supplies,' she went on, more enthusiastic than Romillie had seen her for some time. 'I'll come into town with you in the morning and you can drop me off.'

'You can take the car if you like?' Romillie offered, and smiled as she pointed out, 'It is your car after all.'

But Eleanor was not ready to start driving again yet, it seemed. 'If I'm laden with bags I'll treat myself to a taxi,' she said, and sounded so confident. The change in her was remarkable.

After breakfast her mother went 'sorting things out' in her studio. And, left alone, Romillie had too much time to think. Oh, heavens, was she 'her father's daughter' in that she had inherited his loose morals?

She had been kissed before, plenty of times. And if Jeff Davidson had had his way it would not have stopped at just kissing. He had tried to pressurise her into going back to his place, even to go away with him for a weekend. But, apart from her home situation being such that she would not dream of leaving her mother alone overnight, Romillie had never felt so bowled over by his kisses that she had been in danger of losing her head.

But last night, though, with Naylor! Oh, for heaven's sake, would that memory forever haunt her?

Naylor's first kiss had been angry, and had been meant as a punishment. But his second kiss... Oh, stop it! What was it about him that made him so very special that she could perhaps, under different circumstances, have ended up losing her head?

She tried to think it must be his experience over her relative naivety, but—was it? It wasn't as if she was in love with him or anything of that nature. My stars, she barely knew the man! Which brought her back to that overwhelmingly dreaded nightmare—was she more like her father than she had known? It was a fact that Archer Fairfax could teach a tom cat a thing or two.

Romillie went to bed that night feeling no better than she had when she had left it that morning.

It was only when she was under the shower on Monday morning, having yesterday been constantly torn apart with her worries, that it suddenly hit her like a bolt from the blue that she was nothing at all like her father! She could not possibly be! The relief was tremendous.

She was twenty-three, for goodness' sake! Had she inherited those same 'fast and loose' tendencies, then surely they would have made an appearance before now?

Of course they would! It was not her that was at fault—if to respond to Naylor the way she had *had* been a fault. If blame there be, she could put the blame on Naylor; he with his strong arms and that kiss that had made her want more.

'You're sure you don't want to give me a ring to come and pick you up?' she asked her mother as she dropped her off at the place where she'd used to purchase her art materials. 'I'm sure it wouldn't be any problem getting someone to fill in for me for half an hour.'

'I'm positive,' Eleanor replied, trying to sound confident. 'I'll see you at home at lunchtime.'

With traffic against her, Romillie was a few minutes later than usual in getting to the dental practice. But with her parting from Naylor still in her head, so, as she went to leave her car, she halted.

All at once she realised that as well as an apology for using him to show Jeff Davidson that he wasn't the only eligible male in her orbit, she had reason to not only apologise but to thank Naylor, too. Because had it not been for him—he the instigator of her 'womanly urges'—then she might still be disquieted, as she had been over the years, with fears that she might have some hidden promiscuity gene. Thanks to Naylor, who had triggered her in-depth soul-searching yesterday, she now knew that she had no need to ever worry about it again. It was not promiscuity that had surfaced on Saturday night, but nothing more than proof that she was a normal healthy female of the species.

She had more than that to thank him for, she realised. She guessed he was a busy man, with a busy man's busy social life. Yet, when he might well have had something else planned for Saturday, he had 'honoured' his need to make amends for his earlier accusation that she was selfish, and had generously agreed to accompany her to a kind of function which she guessed was not quite what he normally amused himself with for entertainment on a Saturday evening.

On impulse she took out her phone and rang directory enquiries, and thought for a few seconds only before ringing the number they supplied. At the same time she unearthed her credit card from her bag.

'Sorry I'm late,' she said cheerfully as she went in—Cindy, covering for her, was already knee-deep taking her calls.

'Did you enjoy Saturday?' Cindy replied, the equivalent of *Who was he?*

'I thought it went well. Naylor enjoyed it too,' Romillie answered brightly, and, with the usual heavy load of Monday-morning telephone calls, had no time to chat. Though she hoped as the day wore on that Naylor would enjoy, and not be offended by the peace-making white roses she had sent him.

From the little she knew of him she thought he would not be offended or embarrassed—she had a feeling nothing would faze him—but hoped he would accept the gesture in the way it was meant. She hoped too that, along with seeing the 'Sorry and thank you, Romillie' card that should arrive with them, he would see she was trying to make amends.

She wanted him to think that the 'thank you' was because he had agreed to be her guest—only *she* would know the huge favour he had done her in lifting the sometimes just niggling but at others very disturbing private fears. The 'sorry', although she had apologised once, was no more than he was due.

Romillie did not regret her action when she went home at lunchtime. Her mother seemed to have had an enjoyable shopping expedition, and had been happily employed doing things artistic in her studio.

'Did you come home by taxi?' Romillie asked.

'It did seem an extravagance, but I *was* laden,' Eleanor replied.

'Good.' In Romillie's view, her mother deserved the best.

Though Romillie started feeling pangs of unease when, Lewis Selby having paid their home a visit on Wednesday, she went home on Thursday and learned that he had called again—only this time he had asked her mother to have dinner with him the following evening.

'What do you think?' Eleanor asked.

'What did you tell him?' Romillie prevaricated. She liked Lewis, she really did. But this was her vulnerable, sensitive and, for all her years and experience, gullible as ever mother!

'I said I'd think about it. But I think I'll give him a ring tomorrow and tell him no.'

'You don't like him?'

'Of course I like him. It's years since I met anyone so—sort of—inwardly good.'

Striving to keep her face expressionless, Romillie could not help wondering if her father had started off appearing to be the same 'good' sort of man. Only look what a disaster he had turned out to be!

'Do you want to go?' Romillie asked, which, pushing her anxieties to one side, seemed to be the most important question.

'Seventy-five per cent of me wants to. But—oh, I don't know. I mean, I know it's only dinner, but…'

'You're three-quarters of the way there,' Romillie commented quietly.

She went home on Friday to find that her parent had telephoned Lewis and had agreed to dine with him. But, while most of Romillie applauded this positive step, she at the same time felt the protective one again, and was hard put to it not to give Lewis a call herself and tell him that her mother was very special and not to upset her in any way.

'You look lovely,' she told her, when Eleanor came downstairs and asked if she looked all right.

'You don't think this skirt is too short?' she worried of her knee-length silk two-piece.

'Mother, you're forty-nine, not ninety nine—and with the second-best pair of legs in the world!'

'Just because you've been told you have the best pair—and I'm forty-nine and nine months,' her mother laughed. But it had the desired effect in that she seemed to unwind a little.

She was uptight again by the time Lewis, earlier than he had said, arrived. But, as before, it seemed as if all he had to say was a quiet, 'Good evening, Eleanor,' and she was instantly at ease.

'I shouldn't think we'll be too long,' Eleanor said as she and Lewis were about to leave.

Romillie's anxiety peaked. For the past five years her mother had been hers to watch over, and while part of her applauded this growing confidence in her, she could not help but be concerned over her. 'Take care,' she said lightly, but was looking at Lewis and hoping he understood those two unspoken words—Take care *of her*.

He opened the door for Eleanor to go through, and as if aware of how Romillie was feeling, 'I'll look after her,' he said.

But somehow, an hour after they had gone, Romillie still felt most unsettled. The telephone ringing gave her something else to pin her thoughts on—even if it was only someone interested in selling her something she was not remotely interested in.

The caller was not a double glazing salesperson, however, but, to her surprise, Naylor Cardell! 'Romillie,' he said, and a little frisson of pleasure tingled along her spine.

'Naylor,' she said, knowing his voice immediately.

'I rang to thank you for the roses,' he said, his voice smooth, cultured.

'I—hope I didn't embarrass you.'

'Not at all,' he replied urbanely. 'My first flowers. I was rather tickled, actually.'

'I wanted to say sorry again.'

'You did that beautifully,' he responded—and she thought that was it, that the phone call was at an end.

But she did not want it to end, so rushed in quickly with that which was very much on her mind. 'I'm—er—glad you rang,' she told him breathlessly.

There seemed to be a rather long pause. She did not want to have to say it again. Then found she did not have to when, his voice the same as ever, 'You are?' he enquired.

'Lewis,' she said without preamble. 'He and my mother have gone out to dinner tonight.'

'Yes, I know.'

'He told you?'

'We're colleagues, we work together. We're friends—we chat on all manner of subjects.'

'Mmm. I suppose you would.'

Another small silence, and then quietly, 'What's worrying you, Romillie?' he asked.

'My mother. She hasn't been out with anybody since my father. She's very vulnerable,' she told him quickly. 'I don't want her hurt.'

'Lewis won't hurt her.'

'You can't guarantee that!' she burst out—nobody could.

'I can guarantee his integrity,' Naylor returned unhesitatingly.

It was Romillie's turn to pause. On the face of it she knew she was being ridiculous—it was just one date, for goodness' sake. Yes, but Lewis had been popping in and out for quite some while—and it had been a long road to her mother getting this far.

'Look, you're obviously unsure about Lewis.' She did not answer, and he went on decisively, 'Tell you what, why not meet me for a drink tomorrow, and I'll try and set your mind at rest about him?'

'Oh, you don't need to put yourself out like that…' She began to protest.

'If you're very good, I'll feed you as well,' Naylor said, as if she had not spoken.

'You don't have to…' she began again. 'I mean, my mother might come home tonight and say that she isn't going to see Lewis again.'

'You don't believe that any more than I do,' Naylor stated sternly. 'I'll call for you around seven,' he added. And, before she could again tell him that he did not have to, he was gone.

By the time her mother and Lewis returned Romillie was feeling all sorts of a fool—particularly when both Lewis and her mother were wearing smiles and appeared to have had a splendid evening.

Romillie left her room on Saturday morning with the opinion that she had been worrying over nothing growing bigger and bigger. It bothered her greatly that because of her anxieties she seemed to have somehow inveigled Naylor into giving up yet another of his Saturday evenings.

She felt very much like ringing him and cancelling his kind invitation. A couple of things were against that. She neither had his home telephone number, nor a clue to where he lived. Her mother wouldn't know either, and, even should her mother have Lewis's home telephone number, since he was the subject matter of their meeting anyway, Romillie felt awkward about using him to gain Naylor's phone number.

So, 'Naylor rang while you were out last night,' she informed her mother over breakfast. And, when Eleanor looked at her expectantly, 'I'm—er—having a meal with him tonight.'

With her mother's approval assured, Romillie showered and changed around six. She had no idea where Naylor would take her, and had to admit that part of her was quite excited at the thought of seeing him again.

Though, since their discussion was not likely to last long, it could all be said and done while they sat in his car.

She opted for a pair of fine wool black trousers and a loose top that would be suitable for a meal in a pub or some smart hotel.

Naylor had done away with that 'meet me somewhere' and had said he would call for her around seven, and she was upstairs pulling a brush through her thick and long dark hair when, at five to that hour, she heard his car on the drive.

Feeling a touch nervous for no apparent reason other than she was starting to feel he had made the journey unnecessarily—now that her mother was safe home and none the worse for her dinner with Lewis, but was blossoming in actual fact—Romillie went down the stairs.

Her mother and Naylor were in the sitting room. 'Sorry to have kept you,' Romillie said with a smile, her eyes on the tall man who unfolded his long length from one of the easy chairs. Her heart gave a little bump as he came over to her. He really was too good-looking. She saw his glance go over her, linger for an instant on the lips he had kissed a week ago, and had a feeling he thought that she didn't scrub up too badly either. She dragged her eyes from him. 'I shouldn't think I'll be too late,' she told her parent, much in the same way her mother had said when she had gone out last night.

'Enjoy your evening,' Eleanor instructed, and Romillie knew her 'date' with Naylor had her mother's blessing.

But Romillie had started to feel a bit of a fool again by the time she was seated beside Naylor in his car and heading out of the drive. 'You've come all this way for nothing,' she said on a sudden rush.

'Oh, I wouldn't say that,' he returned easily. And, flicking a glance at her before turning to the front again, 'But why, particularly?' he enquired.

'Our—meeting. You giving up your Saturday evening again. It all seems—sort of fraudulent, somehow.'

'Because?'

'Because… Well, for one thing you'd already told me what a fine man Lewis is. That he's honourable and that my mother would come to no harm with him. But…'

'But?' he encouraged.

'But—my mother has been through a truly terrible time, and I just couldn't think "fine" and "honourable" when she said she was going to have dinner with Lewis. I just wanted to protect her from further hurt if I could—only I couldn't. And I just forgot my own opinion of what a very nice man Lewis is and started to panic a bit.' She had an idea she was gabbling and explaining it all very badly. But Naylor stayed quiet and let her say what she would. 'I'd started to feel a bit stupid even before, all smiles, my mother and Lewis came home.'

'You're not stupid,' Naylor said. 'You're lovely and caring.'

'That's kind of you to say so,' Romillie replied, somehow feeling a little choked-up by his comment. 'But I feel now that I sort of brought you over here under false pretences. Look,' she said suddenly, 'we don't have to go anywhere. You can take me back home if you like.'

He laughed, a natural spontaneous laugh. 'No way!' he said forthrightly.

'No way?'

'It's gone seven on a Saturday night—all the prettiest girls will be taken by now,' he drawled, and she wasn't sure whether he was joking or otherwise. 'Besides which, you can spend some of the evening explaining to me what's going on between you and Davidson.'

'Jeff?'

'One and the same,' Naylor replied, and just then pulled up at a smart restaurant. 'I hope you're hungry,' he said as he parked his car. 'The food here is said to be good.'

It was good. But, when from his remark she would have thought he would say more about Jeff Davidson, they were coming to the end of their second course before his name cropped up again. Up until then Naylor had steered the conversation in many directions. And she really had to admire him. She supposed it was all part of the man that he made it seem as if he wanted to know every facet of her. What girl wouldn't feel flattered? Even though she was sure he had done this dozens of times.

Romillie had just eaten the last morsel of her beef carbonnade when she looked up to find his eyes on her. 'Davidson,' he said quietly, just that and nothing more, and she knew then that he had not forgotten and that he had always intended to find out more. And, after the way she had used Naylor—more to show Jeff Davidson that she really did have a male guest to bring to that dinner rather than that she wanted Naylor to accompany her—she knew that he merited an explanation.

'You've not forgiven me?' she asked, looking into his steady, waiting blue eyes.

'I'll let you know,' Naylor answered.

And Romillie drew a long breath. 'I used to go out with Jeff,' she revealed.

'I guessed there was some sort of history,' Naylor put in, his striking blue eyes giving nothing away of his thoughts. Though his tone had sharpened when he suddenly demanded, 'Do you still go out with him?'

'No!' she exclaimed. 'Nor would I ever again.'

'Oh, my word, that sounds totally final,' he murmured. 'What did he do to deserve such harsh treatment?'

Romillie had no idea if Naylor was serious or not. But decided to take his question as a serious one. She shrugged. 'I don't date more than one person at a time—it's just something I don't do.'

'Very proper.'

'You think I'm a fool?' she flared, guessing that he juggled half a dozen females at one and the same time.

'You mustn't presume to know what I think,' Naylor replied urbanely. And broke off just then because the waiter had arrived to clear their dishes and enquire of their last course.

They both ordered cheese, which gave Romillie chance to cool down again. Indeed, she was beginning to wonder what it was about this man that he could have her smiling one minute and rearing up at him at the next. Or was it not him, but her? It was true she had never been out with anyone quite like him before.

'Do I gather that Davidson was dating someone else while you were going out with him—and you found out?'

She nodded. 'One of the dental nurses.'

'He told you?'

'She did—she's rather a nice girl, actually. Cindy—you may remember her. Blonde…' She had no need to go further. Naylor remembered her from the dinner, of course he did.

'She may have been telling fibs,' Naylor suggested.

'She wasn't. I asked him.'

'Along with the words,"You're dumped"?'

She had to laugh. 'Not quite,' she replied, aware of his glance to her up-tilted mouth. 'He said he hadn't known that he was mine exclusively. I told him that he wasn't—and cancelled our date for that evening.' She broke off. 'Why am I telling you all this?'

'Because I wanted to know. So you never went out with him again?'

Romillie shook her head. 'But I see him every work day. I had been going to go to Alex Yardley's retirement dinner with him, but when Jeff had the nerve to ask if it was still on I told him I was going with someone else.'

'Only that someone else couldn't make it?' Naylor queried. 'Or was I your intended?' he asked, raising an eyebrow.

'Stop making me laugh—I don't intend to ever have an intended!' she said lightly. 'Actually, I had my mother in mind when I said it. But when I asked her she wasn't keen, and suggested I ask you.'

'That's how I was elected?'

'Not really. I'd have been quite happy to have gone on my own, but Jeff Davidson started to make it plain that he didn't think I'd got a partner, so...'

'So it became a point of honour that you take someone?'

'Something like that,' she agreed. And, looking across at Naylor, found she was saying, 'Actually you're better-looking than he is, and he wasn't last in the queue when good-looks were handed out.'

'Are you making a play for me?' Naylor demanded.

She looked at his wonderful mouth with its upward curve and knew that he was teasing, and had to laugh again. But she confessed, 'I didn't like you at first. But now...'

'But now you do?'

'Yep,' she agreed, feeling a bit of an idiot. 'Anyway,' she rushed on, to cover a moment of feeling awkward, 'it was only when I was trying to get hold of Lewis—I'd phoned before, but he was in a meeting, and when he wasn't in the building the next time I rang—I found I was asking for you. And there you were, saying if there was anything you could do to make amends for the tough way you were with me when we first met, and, probably because my mother had put your name in my head, I—um—asked you.'

'Always happy to oblige,' he said, looking into her eyes. 'Shall we have coffee in the lounge?'

Romillie had thought that, their meal finished, he would take her home. But all at once she knew that it was true—she did like him. Enough to want to extend the evening, anyhow. 'I'd like that,' she agreed.

Though when, after one cup of coffee, she took a glance at her watch, she was amazed at how the time had flown.

'More coffee?' Naylor enquired as a waiter hovered.

Romillie felt she would have liked to prolong the evening. But there was not only herself to consider. 'It's been a lovely evening,' she replied openly, 'but I think I should like to go home.'

They were in his car, driving towards her home, when Naylor asked casually, 'Anyone else since Davidson?'

Somehow or other, having been so open with Naylor that evening, she almost said, Only you. But their relationship was not of the same manfriend-womanfriend kind she had thought she had shared with Jeff. So, 'No,' she replied, and, still open with Naylor, 'Not that I've had so many semi-serious boyfriends.'

'You always like to be home before the clock strikes twelve,' Naylor observed.

She almost asked how he had known that, but what he did not know she was beginning to think he was sharp enough to pick up on. He must know by now, she supposed, that her mother was her first priority.

'Some men put up with it, others don't,' she answered lightly.

'And it doesn't matter much if they don't?'

'Something like that,' she agreed.

'Davidson still knocking at your door?'

'He's not coming in,' she said with a laugh.

She turned her head to glance at Naylor, saw that a smile was lurking around his mouth too, and had felt never more content all at once.

Then she saw his smile fade, but his manner was still casual when he commented lightly, 'Not that I think you should take

up with Davidson again, but what happened, Romillie, to make
you so unforgiving?'

'I'm not unforgiving!' she exclaimed. But, more slowly,
'Am I?' she asked. And somehow, perhaps from the respect she
had for Naylor, she found she was telling him, 'I've absolutely
no intention of being treated, or risking being treated, in the
same way my father treated my mother!' And, feeling all hot
and bothered suddenly—family matters were private—'What
is it about you?' she exploded abruptly, 'I just don't share that
sort of thing with anyone!'

'My winning ways?' he suggested—and, maddeningly, he
had made her want to laugh again.

'Anyhow, I owe you a debt of gratitude,' she confessed—
there seemed little point in holding back now.

'You do?'

Glancing from him, she saw that they had arrived at her
home, and as Naylor steered his car up the drive she started to
have second thoughts.

Only at the top of the drive he halted the car and switched
off the engine, but instead of getting out he turned to her and
asked, 'You're not going to leave it there, are you?'

She knew that, she having stated that she owed him, he
wanted to hear more. But she was very unsure then that she
wanted to *say* more. 'Forget I said anything,' she tried.

But he wasn't having that. 'Now I really *am* interested,' he
replied, and, stretching out a hand, he gently stroked the back
of it down the side of her face. 'Come on, little one,' he said
softly. 'You know full well I'm not going anywhere until you
tell me what I'm starting to think is some enormous dark cloud
you're battling with.'

Romillie looked at him, amazed again by his sensitive in-
tuition that had first shown itself that night they had gone out
in a foursome—and found she was revealing, 'That, in part, was
what the flowers were about.' This time Naylor stayed silent,

'It—they,' she felt compelled to continue, 'were a kind of thank-you for—um—lifting that dark cloud that had been hanging over me from time to time ever since I was able to comprehend such matters.'

'Go on,' Naylor encouraged gently when she seemed to struggle for words.

She hesitated, but then found her voice again, quiet though it was. 'I—used to wonder, not all the time, but too frequently for comfort, if I had inherited some kind of promiscuous gene from my father.' And, having said so much, 'He'd make a libertine seem like a saint,' she added.

'And you thought you were like him?' Naylor asked sceptically, and Romillie just loved that note of disbelief in his voice.

'I've never talked to anyone about this,' she confessed huskily.

'Then it's more than high time you did,' he replied, and although encouraging he was unsmiling, and she knew that he meant it.

She turned from him to stare unseeing at the front window of the car. 'As I said, it has bothered me on and off for years now, haunted me that I might turn out to be like him. But then, last Saturday, you got angry with me, and kissed me—'

'Not a very pleasant kiss,' Naylor cut in.

'True,' she agreed. 'But then you kissed me again, a different kind of kiss, and…'

'And?'

'And I started to worry.'

'It troubled you that I held you in my arms?' he asked sharply.

'No. no. Not that!' she said quickly. He had sounded a touch upset. 'It wasn't that. What worried me was the fact that it seemed like only two minutes since I'd finished with Jeff Davidson, yet here I was in another man's arms, and in that second kiss not backing off at first, but…'

'Enjoying the experience?' Naylor queried.

If only he knew. But no way, as open with him as she was

being, could she tell him of the feelings of wanting him that he had stirred in her. 'I wouldn't go that far,' she replied with a light laugh. 'But I didn't find your—your embrace as repugnant as I believed I should. Not just you,' she added quickly.

'But any man, given that you'd only just shaken off Davidson's arms?'

'You don't want to hear all this!' she suddenly came to her senses to exclaim. Good grief, Naylor was a man of the world, used to sophisticated women who matched his sophistication.

'Yes, I do,' he contradicted.

But if he thought that as he needed to hear it she needed to tell it, to get it out of her system, Romillie all at once felt shy. Which surprised her when she had been so open with him. Must be something about the man, she concluded, but suddenly she wanted it all quickly said and done.

'So then I started to worry again that I might be like my father.' She struggled to push shyness aside. 'And all the next day this big black cloud followed me around until—probably because I'd most likely worried it to death—it all at once came to me on Monday morning that I couldn't possibly be in the least like my father with his countless infidelities, that I could not possibly have inherited that particular gene.' She turned to Naylor, feeling so much better all of a sudden. 'And that relief was so tremendous I sent you some thank-you flowers.'

'So you did,' he murmured. And, when it was clear she had said all that she intended to say, 'But you've missed something out,' he pressed.

'I haven't.'

He was not to be put off. 'You missed out the bit in between. The part between how after that kiss you worried about it until it came to you that you could not possibly be like your father and the part where you sent me flowers?' Still she had nothing more to say. 'What made you so certain, Romillie?' he asked quietly.

She turned towards the door, had her hand on the handle

ready to leave the car. But somehow, when Naylor made no move to stop her leaving, she discovered that she did not want to part from him on a sour note. Her hand fell away from the door handle and she turned back.

'My father's affairs are legion,' she stated jerkily. 'But I'm twenty-three and I've never had a single one.' She could feel herself going a little bit pink. 'Wouldn't you say that—'

'You're saying you've never been to bed with a man?' Naylor cut in, his expression, in the light shining into the car from the porch lamp, little short of incredulous.

'Is that so very bad?' she bridled, feeling embarrassed suddenly, and wishing she had followed through her intention and left him sitting there.

'You're a virgin?' he demanded, not letting up.

She was starting to get fed up with him, for all she had started this by opening up to him the way she had. 'Yes,' she snapped belligerently, 'I am!'

'Oh, Romillie,' Naylor murmured, and, a smile coming to his otherwise stern expression, 'That's a terrible thing to say to a man.'

In spite of herself, she was intrigued. 'Why?' she stayed with him long enough to ask.

'Hell, sweetheart,' he replied softly, 'either said man will take it as a challenge, and want to personally find out if you're telling the truth—or said man will drop you like a hot brick.'

Romillie stared at him, and all at once as her crossness with him evaporated into thin air he seemed very dear to her. 'So—this was our farewell dinner,' she said—and loved it when he laughed.

But even as she had just started to be aware that she was very attracted to him, Naylor was saying, 'Come on, it's time all good girls were in bed.' He did not stay long after that but, standing in the porch with her, asked, 'You feel all right, Romillie? Not worried about anything?'

'Not a thing,' she told him honestly.

'Then I'll say goodnight,' he said and, looking down at her, he bent and gently kissed her.

Romillie turned from him and went indoors. Naylor Cardell seemed to her then to be a most extraordinary man. She was a private person, she knew that she was, but here she had been, telling him things she had not even told her mother!

She went upstairs to bed, knowing that she had seen the last of him. And somehow she could not help but feel sorry about that.

# CHAPTER FOUR

THE memory of Naylor's kiss, its gentleness, was with her all of the next day. Romillie could only guess she must have a dreamy kind of look on her face when her mother, having already enquired if she'd had a nice time last night, suddenly suggested, 'You really like Naylor, don't you?'

About to tell her that she would not be seeing him again, Romillie all at once recalled what she could only think of as her mother's fear that she was wary of men. 'He's...' she began, then realised that for no particular reason she was blushing, and, simply because it was true, accepted, 'Yes—he's quite unlike any man I've ever met.'

She straight away realised that she had given her mother the wrong impression when her parent smiled as if her answer had pleased her, and tactfully said nothing more. Romillie knew then that her mother now thought she was quite taken with him, but saw that to add anything more now would make an even bigger issue of it than she already had.

So she stayed quiet, and the week progressed, with Jeff Davidson growing more and more intent on getting her to go out with him again. Not a day went by, it seemed, when he did not invite her to join him, be it cinema, theatre, or dinner. Brick wall and head-banging came to mind. But his persistence had started to get her down. So much so that she began to think that if she could find another job within the same easy reach of her home she would seriously consider it.

If, however, she was thinking of changing her job in order to get away from Jeff, who was now beginning to be something of a pest, matters at home were very much brighter.

Lewis had been for his first sitting, spending quite some hours with her mother while Eleanor did some preliminary sketches. He had still been there one evening when Romillie arrived home from work, and her fears that he might hurt her mother had eased considerably. Romillie was starting to accept that Lewis Selby was a vastly different man from her father.

She found she was thinking more and more of Naylor as the days passed. And, having been certain that their paths would never cross again, she was both surprised and delighted when he rang her at the dental surgery on Friday afternoon. Having just turned down a date with Jeff Davidson, it was an extra pleasure to talk to someone who had not the smallest interest in trying to get her to go out with him.

'This is a nice surprise,' she answered his greeting. And, knowing he would be too busy to just ring up for a chat, 'What can I do for you?'

'Did anyone ever tell you—you have the sweetest mind?'

She glowed. 'Not recently,' she answered with a light laugh, and waited for Naylor to tell her why he had called, thoughts that it would have something to do with Lewis and her mother floating around in her head.

But—no. 'I need a favour,' Naylor said into the growing silence.

Romillie felt she owed him. Not least for the peace of mind he had given her over her fears of promiscuity. 'Name it,' she invited.

'My sister and her husband are having a party tomorrow evening—they'll be offended if I don't go,' he explained. 'I'd like you to come with me.' Romillie was shaken speechless. That was the last thing she would have thought he had called to say. 'Um—in a non-challenging way, of course,' Naylor added when she had not answered.

From that she knew, if she had not known before, that Naylor was asking her to partner him in a purely platonic way. 'Any special reason?' she enquired, knowing in advance that there was more to it than that.

There was silence at the other end before, after a moment or two, Naylor jogged her memory, though it needed little jogging. 'Remember you invited me to be your guest when you wanted to show Davidson that you really *did* have other fish to fry…?'

He left it there. But he had no need to spell it out. 'You've tried letting someone down gently, but she's not listening?' Romillie guessed, recalling his gentleness with her on occasion, knowing in advance that he would not do it brutally.

'Will you come?' he asked.

'Of course,' she replied without hesitation, though did qualify, 'We won't be too late getting back?'

'Trust me,' he replied, and had no need to say more. There was little more to be said after that. Naylor would not hear of her driving herself to meet him. 'I'll call for you around eight,' he said, and rang off.

Romillie knew that her mother would raise no objection to her going to a party with Naylor, and would most likely applaud the fact she was going out with him.

Though, before she could begin to tell her that she was going to be Naylor's platonic partner at his sister's party, her mother was informing her that she had plans of her own for the following evening.

'Lewis called this afternoon,' she began, more or less as soon as Romillie got in.

'How's it going?' Romillie asked, somehow sensing that her parent was feeling a touch awkward.

'His portrait? Given that the dear man is so self-conscious it takes an age to get him to relax, it's going slowly, but much better than I'd dared to hope,' Eleanor said with a smile, then added in a sudden rush, 'I hope you don't mind, but I've invited him to join us for dinner tomorrow evening.'

'Oh, Mum,' Romillie said gently, seeing the reason for her mother's feeling of awkwardness. No other man's feet had been under their dinner table since Archer Fairfax had walked out. 'I don't mind a bit—not if you don't mind that I won't be here.'

'You won't be here?'

'I'm going to a party with Naylor.' And, at her parent's suddenly worried look, 'You'll manage perfectly well without me.'

Romillie got ready on Saturday evening and admitted to experiencing a few butterflies. In a way she was flattered that Naylor had invited her to his sister's party, even if she did have no illusions as to just why she had been asked. She guessed that he was as private a person as she was, and for him to invite her to meet a member of his family was not something he would do unless he liked her, regardless of his need—in this case to let some clinging female know that he really was otherwise absorbed.

Had it not been for her own experience of Jeff Davidson and his near obsessive pursuit of her, Romillie might have felt she was being a little unkind to the woman in question. But Jeff was becoming very wearying, and if Naylor was having the same sort of problems, then unkindness just did not come into it.

Lewis had arrived just before seven. Naylor arrived closer to seven-thirty than the 'around eight' he had spoken of. 'You're ready!' he said when she answered the door to him. His glance was admiring of her in her dress of blue georgette over darker blue silk, as he explained, 'I thought Lewis and Eleanor might want us out of the way so they can enjoy their meal uninterrupted.'

Lewis must have been in touch with Naylor—or the other way round—since yesterday afternoon, Romillie saw, and smiled at Naylor for his thoughtfulness. 'Come in,' she invited the tall, good-looking man. 'They're both in the kitchen.'

Naylor went through to the kitchen to say hello while

Romillie disappeared upstairs to check her appearance and to try and settle the absurd fluttery sort of sensation that had taken her from the moment she had glimpsed Naylor's car turning into the drive.

She calmed down once they were on their way. She rather thought she had Naylor to thank for that, because he kept up a 'platonic' kind of friendly conversation throughout their journey.

His sister Phyllida was tall, like Naylor, and blonde, like Naylor, and was obviously delighted to see him. 'It seems an age!' she exclaimed, and, turning to Romillie, 'And I'm so glad he's brought you to see us,' she said warmly, taking her hand. 'Come and say hello to Will—he's around here somewhere.'

Will was her husband, a little shorter than his wife, but so pleasant and comfortable to be with that, as the evening wore on, it was no wonder to Romillie that Phyllida had fallen for him.

'All right?' Naylor asked Romillie as they stood together. Will was circulating, having just caught up with his wife.

'They're so happy together, aren't they?' Romillie commented.

'Blissfully,' Naylor replied, and, looking down into Romillie's wide brown eyes, 'It does happen, you know,' he added quietly.

Romillie did not pretend not to know what he meant. 'Happy marriages?' She shrugged, but, because she liked him, she smiled.

'But not for you?' he guessed. 'Marriage?'

'It's a lovely party,' Romillie offered, and silently thanked Naylor that he did not insist on an answer but asked easily, 'Have I introduced everyone?'

As parties went Romillie thought it was a medium rather than a small party—about twenty or so people standing around in small groups, glasses in hand, making occasional sorties to a splendidly prepared buffet table.

Suddenly there was a small stir over by the door. Romillie looked across, but in no time the rather glamorous female, aged somewhere in her early thirties, had searched out Naylor and was making a beeline over to him.

'Naylor!' she cried breathlessly. 'I've only just realised you'd be here. I put my glad rags on straight away.'

'Pleased you did, Sophie,' Naylor replied politely. And, turning to Romillie, 'I don't think you know Romillie.' Sophie's look said she was not particularly bothered about making her acquaintanceship, but Romillie could not help but feel a little breathless herself when Naylor looked warmly down at her and said, 'Darling, this is Sophie Pettigrew.'

Sophie, Romillie could see, did not care for the 'darling' either, but managed to stay pleasant. 'You've known Naylor long?' she enquired.

That was a sticky one. Romillie wasn't certain how long she was supposed to have known him. While sure that Sophie the 'the one', she had no idea if his break-up with her was recent or some while ago. 'We met through a mutual friend,' she replied, and asked, 'Do you live locally?'

There followed five minutes of pleasant 'mingling'-type chat, where Naylor, as if she were special to him, stayed close by.

Thereafter the evening progressed, with everyone seeming to intermingle until somehow Romillie was separated from Naylor. 'Do you work at all?' asked someone she thought was called Charles, but she had been introduced to so many people she wasn't quite sure.

'I work in a dental practice,' she saw no harm in telling him, and had to laugh when, nothing like being unsubtle, he suggested she give him the practice telephone number in case he needed it in an emergency.

Looking away from Charles, she saw Naylor standing some yards away, with Sophie and a woman named Clare. But he was looking at neither of his companions; he was looking straight at her. She had an impression he did not take kindly to her coming to the party with him and then spending time in what appeared to be laughing and flirting with someone else.

For one ridiculous moment she thought he appeared to be a

tinge jealous. But she at once knew just how ridiculous that was. Their relationship, if relationship it be, was platonic and nothing more. And if Naylor had looked a touch out of sorts—he was chatting quite amiably with his companions now—it was obvious to her now, she'd had a second to two to dissect it, that he'd thought she was letting him down on the Sophie front.

'Will you excuse me?' she said nicely to Charles, smiled warmly, and went from him to join Naylor. He wanted her to role-play? She'd role play. She slipped her arm through his and gave it a squeeze. He looked down at her and squeezed back.

'Ready to go, darling?' he asked.

'When you are,' she replied, looking up into his blue eyes that held such a warm light for her that her heart gave a most peculiar giddy flip.

'You're not going?' Sophie protested.

'You can't!' Clare added her protest.

'My word, you certainly know how to make a man feel good,' he murmured charmingly, and all four of them laughed. He took Romillie, his hand on the hand that was through his arm, to say goodnight to their hosts. 'Night, Philly,' he said to his sister, kissing her cheek and shaking hands with his brother-in-law.

Romillie said her thanks and goodnight, and received a kiss from both Phyllida and Will. 'I'm glad you came,' Naylor's sister commented as she went to the door with them, and Romillie had a feeling she really meant it.

'Enjoy yourself?' Naylor asked, once they were in his car and driving away.

'Very much,' Romillie replied truthfully. 'I met some very interesting people.'

'I think they found you interesting too,' Naylor commented.

'Oh, I don't know about that.' She brushed his comment aside. 'I rather expected an historian to be as dull as dull, but that man—um—Adrian was quite fascinating.'

They were silent for a few minutes. But while Romillie was

wondering if she should mention the glamorous Sophie, or tactfully not say a word, Naylor casually enquired, 'I'm guessing Charlie Todd asked you for your phone number?'

She had to laugh. 'Nothing escapes you!'

'Did you give it to him?' he demanded, and that made her cross.

'What do you take me for?' she retorted sharply. 'I thought I was there to convey that *you* were the sunshine of my life!'

'I'm a swine,' Naylor apologised.

'Besides which, I'm sure if he needed emergency dental treatment that urgently, Charles would find a surgery much closer to home.'

'He's pretty obvious, huh?'

'Some.' Her crossness with Naylor died as swiftly as it had been born.

'How about Davidson?' Naylor enquired. 'Managed to shake him off yet?'

'Don't remind me,' Romillie replied. 'He just isn't getting the message.'

'He's really bothering you?' Naylor asked, not sounding as though he cared for that too much.

'If he gets too bad, I'll find a job elsewhere,' she said lightly, and since Naylor had asked about Charles Todd, not to mention Jeff Davidson, Romillie felt it gave her leave to ask about Sophie. 'I—er—it *was* Sophie, wasn't it? The one who— er—' She broke off, searching for a polite way to put it.

'Sophie has been married and divorced twice,' Naylor filled in. 'I'm hoping that by now, as lovely as she is, Sophie appreciates I've no intention of being husband number three.'

That took Romillie aback slightly. Not that she was shaken to hear Sophie had already parted from two husbands. No, what took her a little aback was that Naylor had sounded for all the world as though he had no intention of being a husband to any female!

'You're—against marriage?' she asked.

'Did you think it was your prerogative?' he countered.

'No, but...'

'Marriage is all right—for other people,' Naylor stated.

Romillie fell silent. She hadn't thought about it, but supposed that had Naylor been marriage-minded he would have found himself a wife by now. But somehow, even as she recalled how on the evening they had met he had said he was completely unattached—and liked it that way—the notion that he viewed marriage for himself in much the same way she viewed it for *herself* just did not sit right with her; and she had absolutely no idea why that should be so.

She had given up thinking about it by the time Naylor turned the car into the drive of her home. She was inwardly smiling suddenly when she realised that—with both of them feeling the way they did about the married state—they were safe with each other.

Which made it odd that, as they stood in the porch and Naylor said, 'Thank you for coming with me tonight, Romillie, I really appreciate it,' holding her briefly by her upper arms as he bent down and kissed her cheek in much the same brotherly fashion that he had kissed his sister, that did not suit her either.

'Any time, Naylor,' she said lightly, and went indoors wondering why, when she was glad that they were 'safe with each other', she should feel a touch miffed at his brotherly kiss.

She had other matters to dwell over when she joined her mother downstairs on Sunday morning. 'Have a nice time last night?' Eleanor asked, setting the kettle to boil.

'Lovely,' Romillie replied. 'How was your dinner?'

'Fine, fine,' her mother replied, but sounded just that little bit abstracted, and Romillie, who knew her so well, knew she was worrying about something.

'What's wrong, Mum?' she asked quietly.

'Nothing—exactly,' Eleanor replied, but sank down onto a kitchen chair. 'Lewis is a dear, a love, but...'

Romillie took a chair opposite her. 'But?' she coaxed.

'Oh, Rom, I don't know. Lewis has asked me to go and spend a few days at his home with him next week.'

Whoa, Lewis, too fast, Romillie knew straight away. 'Are you going?' she asked evenly, aware of the answer in advance. Her mother did need to get out more, that was true. And her friendship with Lewis might have grown and grown. But, after what she had been through, Romillie could not see her leaving the security of her own four walls for a few days in a hurry.

'No, of course not,' Eleanor replied without hesitation.

'But you'd like to—like to spend some time with Lewis in different surrounds?'

'He's—good to be with. He makes me feel less of an apology for a woman than I—'

'Mother!' Romillie cut in, shocked, knowing she had her father to thank that he had reduced her mother to thinking like that. 'Please don't talk that way. After all you've had to put up with—'

'That's in the past. Gone now. I'm over all that,' Eleanor said. 'Well, mainly,' she qualified.

'But, even though you like Lewis very much, you don't feel you can trust him not to turn out like my father?'

'Lewis is nothing at all like your father,' Eleanor said firmly. 'And I do trust him. And he made a point of saying I would have my own room—but it isn't on.'

'You'd like to go, though?'

'Some time, perhaps,' Eleanor replied.

And Romillie let it go. While she was starting to grow more and more confident that perhaps Lewis would put her mother's interests before his own, she knew better than to pressure her.

That did not stop her from worrying about her, though. Perhaps after all it *was* time for her mother to break through a few self-imposed barriers? She had progressed dramatically since knowing Lewis—even to the extent of taking up commissioned work again.

Romillie was still musing over it on Wednesday, as she tidied up her workstation at the end of her stint for the day. Maybe she should have encouraged her mother to accept Lewis's invitation. Surely by now Lewis knew the situation and would look after her.

When Romillie was not thinking of her mother, she found she was thinking of Naylor. She had enjoyed the party last Saturday, had enjoyed being with him. She wondered briefly if anything had happened in his life to have put him off marriage. But, while she did not doubt he knew quite a few divorced people—look no further than her mother, Lewis, or twice-divorced Sophie to name but a few—Romillie did not think it was fear of divorce that kept him single. Much more probable was the fact that Naylor was having too much of a good time being a bachelor to want to settle down.

Suddenly, Romillie discovered she did not like the thought of him having 'too much of a good time'. Too much of a good time, in her view, meant with members of the opposite sex. With a start of surprise Romillie realised she was—jealous!

Good heavens! That was a bit of a shaker! They were good friends, nothing more. Did she actually begrudge him having fun, relaxing, after the hard work he must put in at Tritel Incorporated? She could not believe it, but…

'You can't be busy every weekend.' Jeff Davidson came in to block her exit from the cubbyhole of the reception area.

'It could well be, Jeff, that I just don't want to go out with you!' she said bluntly, and, rude or not, grabbed hold of her bag and forced her way past him. The man was becoming more than a nuisance.

Feeling in something of a sour mood, Romillie pushed through the outer door of the practice and went quickly down the step—only for her mood to immediately lighten. At first she thought her eyes were playing tricks on her—just lately most tall, fair-haired men seemed to morph, if only for an instant, into Naylor. But this time it *was* him. Tall and straight and, if she wanted more proof, standing in the car park next to the car she had ridden in last Saturday.

Unable to keep a wide grin off her face, she walked over to him. 'As I live and breathe, Naylor Cardell!' she exclaimed, and loved it when his wide grin matched hers. 'You're not doing a Charlie Todd on me?'

'I'll have you know, madam, I have no use for emergency dental services,' Naylor replied, and asked, 'How goes it?'

'As well as can be expected,' she replied. 'But I'm starting to wonder what you're doing here.'

'Lewis tells me he's invited Eleanor to his home, but that she has declined.'

'Does he tell you everything?'

'I doubt it,' Naylor replied equably, going on, 'We had to attend a most boring business dinner last evening—and had to talk about something to cheer ourselves up.'

Romillie liked that. Lewis talking of her mother in terms of someone who brightened his load. 'Mum won't go,' she stated.

'You've put her off the idea.'

'*No!*' Romillie protested indignantly. He had come all this way to have a go at her for putting a spoke in his friend's 'courting' wheel, if courting it be? Let him try!

'But you would mind if she went?' Naylor persisted.

Having been so pleased to see him, Romillie was starting to feel decidedly scratchy with the man. 'I want her to be happy,' she stated flatly. 'My mother has been through hell; and this, Lewis's invite, is obviously too soon. She needs time to adjust to someone being—er—interested in her.'

'Lewis has been through his own hell,' Naylor commented. 'But from what I can see, after years in a soulless wilderness, he is more keen than just plain interested.' He thought for a moment, and then brought out, 'I think it would do them both good to have space together in a neutral environment. How would it be if I invited Eleanor to my place for the weekend?'

Romillie blinked. 'Your place?' she queried, just a little short of open-mouthed.

'She'd accept, wouldn't she, if she thought she was doing it for her daughter's benefit?'

Her jaw definitely did drop. 'You've lost me somewhere!' she confessed. 'How did *I* come into this?'

'Well, naturally you'd be there too, with Lewis and Eleanor, otherwise it would make the neutral ground uneven.'

'Sorry to be obtuse, but what are you actually saying?'

'Am I going too fast for you?' Naylor asked with a gentle smile, and went on to make it clearer. 'I propose that I invite you to my place—say Friday to Sunday. Which, because of the worry your mother may have that you have a bit of a hang-up about men, she will applaud.' Romillie's eyes were growing wider by the second. 'But you, dear Romillie, will refuse to come and leave your mother alone for two nights on her own. So I say bring your mother along too.'

'You do?' Romillie asked faintly.

'I do. Further, in order that your lovely mother will not feel she's playing gooseberry to you and me, I'll invite Lewis to keep her company.'

At which point Romillie just had to burst out laughing; she had never heard anything like it. 'You're not serious!' she gasped.

'The sacrifices I'm prepared to make,' Naylor sighed. 'And you did tell me that you thought your mother was growing fond of Lewis.'

'Did I?' Romillie had no recollection of that. But, having stated that she had, Naylor did not repeat it. But Romillie felt obliged to tell him straight, 'I wouldn't like to lie to my mother.'

'You wouldn't have to,' he countered. 'Just tell her I've invited you both to my place, and also that I intend asking Lewis too.'

'You don't know that Lewis will accept.'

'He will.'

'I don't even know where you live.' Romillie was still protesting, probably because now that she had taken on board what he was saying his invitation was starting to have some appeal.

'I've a small *pied-à-terre* in London, but my main home is in the Cotswolds.'

Oh, heavens, a few days in the Cotswold Hills was tremendously tempting. 'I—um…'

'Would you prefer I invited your mother personally?' Naylor offered.

'No, no. I'll do it,' she said quickly—and only then realised that she had just more or less accepted his invitation. 'I'll—er—give you a ring,' she mumbled, and would have walked away. But Naylor, glancing over the top of her head, switched his glance back to her and caught a hold of her arm.

'Is Davidson still bothering you?' he asked.

She guessed from that that Jeff Davidson had just left the building and was walking to the parking area. 'I'm thinking of laying down rat poison,' she answered.

Naylor smiled into her eyes, but all at once his head was coming down. 'Then perhaps, sweet Millie, I'd better say *adieu* properly,' he murmured. And the next she knew he had taken her in his arms and his lips were over hers in a kiss no one could mistake as brotherly.

Not that he made a meal of it, and it was decorous enough not to be embarrassing to an onlooker—but long enough not to be mistaken for anything but a fond parting.

Romillie's heart was racing when she took a shaky step back from him. 'You're too good to me, Cardell,' she muttered, and turned abruptly about, the feel of Naylor's strong arms still about her, the feel of his magnificent mouth on hers still lingering. She saw Jeff Davidson, but blindly *didn't* see him. She did not acknowledge him anyway, but found her car key and unlocked her car.

Feeling all over the place as she drove home, she knew that it was going to take every ounce of tact to get her mother to leave their home for the weekend.

But to her surprise, when she explained that Naylor had come to the dental surgery to extend his invitation, mentioning that Lewis would be there too—and adding that she would not go without her—her mother agreed with very little hesitation!

That was when Romillie realised the full extent of her mother's worry about her offspring's inability to form any sort of long-term relationship. For it seemed that in order that her daughter might further her friendship with Naylor, her mother was even prepared to overcome her unwillingness to leave the security of her own home.

'You're sure?' Romillie pressed. 'We don't have to go if you...'

'I'm looking forward to it already,' Eleanor replied, and, noticing the enthusiasm, the life, in her mother's eyes, Romillie could only be pleased. She rather thought that she herself was looking forward to the Cotswolds weekend too.

She rang Naylor the next day. 'What time would you like us to arrive tomorrow?' she asked when she was put through to him.

'I'll drive you down,' Naylor replied.

But Romillie did not want that. She was as certain as she could be that the weekend would go well, but just in case they had to cut their visit short she wanted to be able to bring her mother home without having to put anyone out.

'It will be better if we come in our car, but thank you for the offer,' she said politely.

'It will be all right, Romillie,' Naylor assured her, every bit as if he knew what going through her mind.

'I'm sure it will. Er—my mother says she is looking forward to it.'

'But not you?' he queried.

'In actual fact, yes, me too,' Romillie told him honestly.

'But this isn't about me. It's about my mother and Lewis having some unpressured time together.'

'Lewis will be delighted when I tell him Eleanor has agreed,' Naylor said smoothly and, a busy man obviously, gave Romillie his Cotswolds address and directions on how to find Oaklands. 'You'd better have my phone number there too—just in case you get lost *en route*,' he added.

'I'll—we'll see you Friday, then,' Romillie said.

'Make it as soon as you can. Before dinner,' Naylor instructed before she could end the call.

'Look forward to it,' she answered, and rang off, knowing it wasn't that Naylor was keen to see her, but that Lewis would be looking out to see her mother—the sooner the better.

Romillie was not in the habit of asking for time off, but, feeling that her mother might start to get jittery the nearer it got to evening, just after lunch on Friday she arranged to leave work an hour early—and was glad to do so.

Jeff Davidson was becoming more than a pain. Word had reached him that she was leaving early, and he bombarded her at every opportunity that afternoon with questions about her relationship with Naylor Cardell and what he had got that Jeff hadn't.

She left work promptly at four, aware that the pest of a man was really getting her down. Were her circumstances different she would leave without waiting to find another job.

Trying to push distressing feelings of being preyed upon from her, and instead start looking forward to the weekend ahead, Romillie turned the car into the drive of her home—only for her spirits to plummet deeper. There on the drive stood her father's car! Nothing good ever came from his visits!

Braking hard, she was out of the car in an instant, already rushing for the door. She could hear him shouting before she had the door open. 'Don't give me that!' she heard him bellowing as she charged towards the sitting room.

Archer Fairfax had not heard her come in—she was not surprised, the way the was roaring. But, to her utter disbelief, the sight that met her eyes was of her bully of a father actually raising his hand to her petrified mother.

In a flash Romillie was over by her mother, standing in front of her. 'Leave her alone!' she yelled, enraged. She had never stood up to him so angrily before, but was now being ruled by a temper she had not previously known she possessed.

He turned his wrath on her, but his hand did drop as loudly he demanded, 'Where do you keep your money?'

'I haven't got any,' she told him furiously, her chin jutting angrily, feeling so outraged just then that if she'd had any spare cash she wouldn't have given it to him anyway.

'I've given you all we have,' her mother broke in shakily. 'Please, Archie, just go. Leave us alone.'

'You do as I say,' he addressed his ex-wife. 'You get to the solicitors first thing on Monday morning and see about selling this house.'

'I'll see my mother goes to the solicitors on Monday,' Romillie erupted, infuriated. 'To see about getting an injunction, restraining you from coming here ever again.'

'Why, you...!' he roared, his hand coming up as though to strike her.

But from a furnace of fury an icy coldness suddenly came over Romillie. 'Do it!' she invited. 'But you lay just one finger on either of us and you'll find yourself spending this weekend in the police cells.'

His hand fell away—and it was over. Just like that it was over. He had no idea if his daughter would actually carry out her threat, but he had protested vociferously when somehow or other the fact that he was being sued for divorce had been reported in the local paper. It would not suit him at all to read that the police had charged him with assault.

Without speaking to either of them again he slammed out—leaving his ex-wife in pieces. Romillie, starting to shake, followed him from the room to the outer door, where she locked and bolted the door. She went back to the sitting room to find her mother in floods of tears. She felt pretty much like crying herself.

'Don't, love, he's not worth it,' she soothed, tears stinging her own eyes. She put an arm around her mother's shoulders—they were both shaking. Romillie was aware then that, within minutes, Archer Fairfax had wiped out months of her mother's gradual surfacing from his despicable treatment of her.

Ten minutes later her mother had recovered sufficiently for Romillie to be able to leave her and go and make a pot of tea. She returned with a tray and poured out two cups.

'How long had he been here?' she asked, sitting beside her on the sofa.

'Long enough to demand I find a way of selling the house. He knows full well it's tied up in trust for you, but still he persists…'

It was plain that he was broke again. Knowing him, probably in debt up to his ears! For herself, Romillie would let him have the house rather than have him upset her mother the way he did every time. But it was not him she had to think about. Her mother had started to paint in her studio again, and anyway they had to have a roof over their heads. Besides which, money burned a hole in his pocket, and he'd be through whatever amount he received in no time.

Her mother must have been thinking of money too, because, 'I'm sorry, Rom, but he was shouting so—I gave him all the money we had. I know that the money in the savings jar was put aside to pay the gas, electricity and phone bills, and the council tax too, but I thought it would be worth it just to get rid of him.'

'It's not important,' Romillie assured her, hiding her feelings of panic, her head a quagmire. That money was all the money they had. Anything of value had been sold ages ago! Where on earth was she going to get more money from?

'It didn't do any good, though, did it?'

'He's gone now. Don't worry about it any more,' Romillie

soothed, trying to get her parent on a more even keel, while at the same time wishing, as she had so often in the past, that she had a good and kind father, like other girls, and not the brute she had been landed with.

'I can't go, Rom,' Eleanor said as her tears dried. Her colour was still ashen, though. 'I can't go with you to Naylor's home,' she said apologetically.

'We'll both stay home,' Romillie decided. 'I'll ring Naylor soon and tell him…' She wasn't sure what she would tell him. Family scenes, domestic upsets, were private. And to Romillie it would be just too terribly distasteful to tell Naylor any of what had occurred. 'Shall I make us something to eat?' she offered, knowing that anything she made was going to taste like chaff in her mouth.

'I couldn't eat a thing,' Eleanor refused.

Some while later Romillie went upstairs and took a shower, everything crowding in on her, tears because her father had been about to hit her mingling with the shower water.

Stepping out of the shower, she began to dry herself and tried not to think of the unholy mess they were in financially. No way, no matter how obnoxious Jeff Davidson showed himself to be, could she walk out of her job now.

It was when she had a horrifying flashback of coming home unexpectedly early to find her father about to strike her mother, and shuddering at the memory, that something all at once surfaced in Romillie and she thought—*No!* Ever since she had married Archer Fairfax her mother had been subjected, one way or another, to his tyranny. It had to stop! And stop now! Her mother deserved better. He would not crush her—not this time, or ever again. There was one very kind and gentle man waiting in the Cotswolds to see her mother. And see her, he would!

Donning a robe, Romillie went down the stairs. 'Mum, I've been thinking…'

'So have I, Rom. I'm not being fair to you. You've been looking forward to seeing Naylor…'

'And I've been thinking that if we don't go then my father has achieved probably what he set out to achieve—to continue to make your life miserable for daring to divorce him.'

'So…' Eleanor took a deep breath. 'So we're going, are we, Rom?'

Romillie took a deep breath too, and acknowledged that it was the truth. She *had* been looking forward to seeing Naylor. 'Yes,' she said. 'We're going.'

Her mother smiled bravely. 'We're going to be late. Perhaps we'd better have a snack before we go. We don't want them holding up dinner for us.'

'I'll—um—go and ring Naylor and tell him we're running behind time.'

Naylor answered straight away, and Romillie wondered if he had left work early too. 'Romillie?' he queried, when for the moment she was speechless to know quite what to say.

'Hello,' she managed.

'You're lost?' he guessed.

'We're still at home,' she began—and had her ears assaulted before she could get any further.

'Don't you dare tell me you're not coming!' he cut in sharply.

'Wouldn't dream of it!' she retorted snappily, one way and another having had her fill that day of either nosy and wearyingly bothersome, to bullying and roaring, and now sharply snarling men. But—she made herself calm down—it wasn't Naylor's fault. 'We've been—er—a bit held up,' she explained. 'Would you mind if we arrived after dinner?'

'Problem?' he enquired, his tone changing to one of wanting to help. But how could she tell him? It was all so sordid! She felt choked suddenly. She'd thought she'd had her fill of men—but Naylor, he was different. 'Just get here as soon as you can,' he said, when she had not answered. 'And drive carefully,' he instructed.

Romillie put the phone down, knowing full well that it was

not her he was bothered about going to his home, but his friend Lewis and her mother. But that mattered not. After the painful upset to her mother wrought by her father's visit, Romillie thought that to get her away for the weekend would be just what was needed.

It was going on for nine when they reached the village of Abbots Gordon. Romillie followed Naylor's directions, and half a mile outside of the village came to Oaklands, Naylor's lovely old Cotswold stone house. She steered the car up the long oak-tree-lined drive, quietly admitting to feeling a little churned up. Not all of that was due to her feeling of anxiety brought on by that scene with her father.

'What a lovely house!' her mother exclaimed, admiring the pale gold stonework as they left the car. They both stood back to admire the house and grounds, Eleanor possibly with an artist's eyes, Romillie just liking what she saw.

Then the stout front door was opening—and both Naylor and Lewis were there. 'You made it,' Naylor commented, coming over to them. Whereupon he bent down and laid a light kiss on Romillie's lips. Her heart went bumpity-bump, but she knew that his kiss was for her mother's benefit—just as she knew that there was nothing 'pretend' about the gentle kiss Lewis laid on her mother's cheek.

With Naylor taking charge of Romillie's weekend case, and Lewis taking Eleanor's from her, they moved indoors. And as Romillie glanced about her elegant surroundings, so for the moment she forgot the welter of worry that had refused to be pushed into the background on their journey.

'Your home is beautiful, Naylor,' she said softly as he and Lewis escorted them from the wide hall, past the wide and thickly carpeted staircase and into a high-ceilinged drawing room.

'We've saved you some dinner if…'

'We're not at all hungry,' Eleanor stated. 'We had something to eat before we left.'

No one made mention of why they were later than arranged, but anyone with a discerning eye could see that both mother and daughter were looking a shade pale, and that Eleanor's eyes were a tiny bit red-rimmed.

'Let me show you your rooms,' Naylor suggested, and all four of them went out into the hall and up the magnificent staircase.

It was plain to Romillie that, while doing nothing to detract from the beauty of the building, the inside had been completely updated. They went first along to the room given over to her mother, another high ceilinged, large and airy room with its own *en suite* bathroom.

'You're along the landing this way,' Naylor said to Romillie, and they left her mother chatting to Lewis while Naylor escorted Romillie about four doors down in the opposite direction. 'I hope you'll be comfortable here,' he said, leading the way into a room similar to the one allocated to her mother.

'We've put you to a lot of trouble,' Romillie commented.

'Mrs Jennings, from the village, saw to the domestic side,' Naylor replied, and as he stood looking down into Romillie's troubled velvety brown eyes, 'To have you here is what I wanted, Romillie,' he added quietly.

She knew full well that he did not mean her in particular, but for all that her heart gave that quirky little spurt that was becoming something of a habit since she had known him.

'Come down when you're ready,' he said, and abruptly left her.

Ten minutes later Romillie had unpacked her weekend case and gone along to her mother's room. 'How are you feeling now?' she asked her.

'Much less shaky. I'm glad we came,' Eleanor volunteered, and that pleased Romillie.

They went down the stairs together, and while Romillie still felt on edge—and that had nothing to do with being in Naylor's home—the good manners required of being a guest carried her through the next hour.

Lewis and Eleanor were seated on a most beautiful antique gold sofa when, in answer to Lewis's enquiry of had she had a busy day, setting down her sherry glass Eleanor looked a shade haunted, but managed a smile. 'Fairly busy,' she replied. 'Romillie came home early and—' She stopped dead, and looked frantically to her daughter.

'They were very good, my employers,' Romillie jumped in quickly, if a little jerkily. 'They allowed me to leave an hour ahead of time—but then we lost track of time, didn't we?' She smiled to her mother, and rattled on while her mother got a better grip of herself. 'But all in all it's been a bit—er—busy.' She was running out of steam, and knew it.

'I know it's still relatively early,' Eleanor said, composure regained, 'but would you mind very much if I went up to bed?'

'I'll come with you,' Romillie said, and was on her feet. 'I'll say goodnight,' she said generally, and, intending to wait for her mother, turned towards the door. But she was prevented from taking a step when Naylor, on his feet too, placed an arm lightly over her shoulders.

She was not sure she did not give a little start at the unexpectedness of it. But Naylor held her steady. 'Have a good night,' he bade her softly, his striking blue eyes searching hers. She tried to find her voice, but couldn't. Then any semblance of thought, of thinking, ceased altogether when his head came down and he placed a light kiss on her mouth.

Romillie was still not capable of very coherent thought as she and her mother went up the stairs. Naylor's kisses were disturbing somehow, even though she absolutely knew that they were all part of what this weekend was about.

'Are you all right, Mum?' she asked when they reached the top of the stairs.

'Feeling better with every minute,' Eleanor replied.

That made Romillie feel better too. But away from her parent, away from Naylor and the need to keep up a smiling front, Romillie collapsed on to her bed. Only then did she acknowledge the cost of keeping up the pretence that all was right with her world. It was far from right! Very, very far from right!

With space now to let her thoughts have free rein, Romillie felt battered from all corners. She had Jeff Davidson and his non-stop pursuit of her to face again on Monday. Heaven alone knew how it had grown to become as bad as it had, this drip, drip, drip, wearing away at her.

On top of that she knew that she was going to have to do something about her father—but what? For all her brave talk about getting a restraining order against him she did not know how that could be achieved. To consult a solicitor was going to take money. Money which, thanks to him, they did not have!

Romillie felt humiliated that he had actually raised his hand to her. She felt sickened that he *would* have hit her had she not found the strength from somewhere to stand up to him.

Though far better for him to hit her than her mother. Romillie did not doubt that, had she not arrived home when she had, her bully of a father would have set about his ex-wife.

Feeling drained suddenly, Romillie went through the ritual of washing and getting into her nightclothes. She felt deeply saddened, and as she lay down in bed her head was spinning. All the money that had been set aside to meet their bills had gone!

One thought chased after another as she closed her eyes. Their boiler was on its last legs and would need replacing soon. Without the wherewithal to buy a new one, not to mention the cost of labour to have it installed, it looked like being a very cold winter.

Desperately searching for something, anything at all on which they could raise money, Romillie reluctantly came to their only asset. The car! The road tax and insurance, even without the general maintenance charges, were starting to look like a luxury they just could not afford.

Romillie eventually fell asleep, with such worrying matters

# Get FREE BOOKS and FREE GIFTS when you play the...

# LAS VEGAS

## GAME

7

*Just scratch off the gold box with a coin. Then check below to see the gifts you get!*

## YES! I have scratched off the gold box. Please send me my **2 FREE BOOKS** and **2 FREE GIFTS** for which I qualify. I understand that I am under no obligation to purchase any books as explained on the back of this card.

**316 HDL ENT4**                    **116 HDL ENY4**

|  |  |  |  |  |  |  |  |  |  |  |  |
|---|---|---|---|---|---|---|---|---|---|---|---|

FIRST NAME                          LAST NAME

|  |  |  |  |  |  |  |  |  |  |  |  |
|---|---|---|---|---|---|---|---|---|---|---|---|

ADDRESS

|  |  |  |  |  |
|---|---|---|---|---|

APT.#            CITY

(H-R-01/08)

STATE/PROV.      ZIP/POSTAL CODE

| 7 | 7 | 7 | Worth TWO FREE BOOKS plus TWO BONUS Mystery Gifts! |
|---|---|---|---|
| 🍒 | 🍒 | 🍒 | Worth TWO FREE BOOKS! |
| 🔔 | 🔔 | ☘ | TRY AGAIN! |

**www.eHarlequin.com**

Offer limited to one per household and not valid to current subscribers of Harlequin Romance®. All orders subject to approval.

◄ DETACH AND MAIL CARD TODAY! ▼

**BUSINESS REPLY MAIL**

FIRST-CLASS MAIL    PERMIT NO. 717    BUFFALO, NY

POSTAGE WILL BE PAID BY ADDRESSEE

**HARLEQUIN READER SERVICE**
**3010 WALDEN AVE**
**PO BOX 1867**
**BUFFALO NY 14240-9952**

NO POSTAGE
NECESSARY
IF MAILED
IN THE
UNITED STATES

still whirling around in her head, one thought charging urgently after another. It did not surprise her that she slept only fitfully, nor that she awoke early, feeling not at all rested.

. She glanced around her lovely room and dwelt briefly on thoughts of Naylor, and how vastly different he had shown himself to be from her first impression of him. Unconsciously her hand went to her mouth. He had kissed her—she liked his kisses.

Oh, for goodness' sake! In the next instant Romillie was out of bed. She went over to the window and looked out. Everywhere seemed fresh and green—it had rained in the night, she observed, though rain had been promising all day yesterday. No wonder she liked Naylor's kisses. He had a wonderful mouth.

Oh, grief! Impatiently she checked her watch. Five-thirty. Early, yes, but then she and her mother had gone to bed earlyish.

Having done with sleep, her worries of the previous evening had awoken with her, and seemed to be starting the day as they meant to go on. Romillie, knowing that her early riser mother might be awake too, decided to tiptoe along to her room and check how she was faring.

Donning her lightweight wrap, and mindful of the occasional creaky wooden floorboard in old houses, Romillie tiptoed from her room. But even though she was being careful she did manage to find one creaky floorboard. At that same moment she noticed that one of the bedroom doors was quite ajar. But before it could more than just register that either Naylor or Lewis must prefer to sleep with their bedroom door open, Naylor himself, hastily tying up a robe, appeared.

'Romillie.' He said her name quietly, and she guessed he did not want to disturb his other guests should they—rightly, at this hour—still be asleep.

'I'm sorry,' she whispered back, shaken, pleased, but feeling a bit bewildered to see him. 'I was just going along to ch-check on my mother. That is…' She added confusion to the list, and, it being too early in the day to dissemble, heard herself say,

'We—had a bit of an upset yesterday…' Her voice tailed off. 'S-sorry to have disturbed you,' she said quickly, and hurried along to her mother's room.

Because of the early hour she entered her mother's room without knocking, and was glad she did when she saw that her mother, probably emotionally exhausted from yesterday, was still sound asleep. Good.

Naylor was nowhere to be seen when she retraced her steps. His bedroom door was closed and she began to feel guilty that she had disrupted his slumbers.

But Romillie was feeling much, much worse a few minutes later when, not wanting to wake the whole house if the shower and plumbing were anywhere near as noisy as the plumbing in her old home, she opted to study the view from the window seat.

She did not get to study the view just then, however, because as she perched knees raised, intending to place her feet on the ledge, horrified, she saw that her feet were not the same clean and presentable feet she had slipped between the bedcovers last night. Her feet were, in fact, filthy! They were the feet of someone who had been walking on wet ground!

In an instant the years rolled away. And she knew in that instant what had happened. The last time she'd had feet like that had been the last time she had taken a walk outside—in her sleep. She gave an inner groan—oh, perish it, she had been sleepwalking!

Romillie was still striving to come to terms with the fact that she, a guest in someone else's house, while everyone else was asleep, had resumed again that childhood habit that seemed to be associated with her father shouting and roaring about the place. But just then something almost equally alarming struck her.

She recalled Naylor's quietly spoken 'Romillie' just now. His voice had been quiet, she had thought, so as not to disturb his other guests, who might well be sleeping. But had it been that? Or had he said her name quietly like that so as not to disturb her or jar her awake had she been sleepwalking?

Oh, heavens! Romillie played back in her mind's eye she and her mother coming up those stairs last night and reaching the landing. Naylor's bedroom door had not been open or ajar then, she would swear it, so it was *not* his habit to leave it that way.

She recalled the speedy way that he, knowing the noises of his home better than anyone, had been out of that door like a shot the moment she had stepped on that creaky floorboard.

Feeling hot all over, Romillie knew then, for sure, that at whatever time it was that she had gone 'walkabout' Naylor had witnessed it. And that was why his door had been ajar! So that he—a light sleeper, obviously—would hear her if she went walkabout again. And, but for her grubby feet from her barefoot walk in the rained-on ground, she would never have known.

And—she loved him.

In that moment of realising that Naylor, silently and without fuss, had been protecting her, Romillie knew what had been stirring in her heart for him for what seemed like a long while now. She was in love with him. No trumpets, no alarm bells to warn her—she was in love with him. It was just there.

All of her other problems—Jeff Davidson, her father, their lack of money, even her sleepwalking—paled into insignificance in those first few minutes of Romillie finally facing and acknowledging that which was now inescapable. She was in love with Naylor. But equally inescapable was the fact that there was absolutely and utterly no possible future in it.

# CHAPTER FIVE

HAD her mother not come along to ask if she was ready to go down to breakfast, Romillie would have happily done without breakfast.

'Ready when you are,' she answered cheerfully, but her mind was in a whirl. 'Did you get off to sleep all right?' she asked as together they went down the stairs.

'That's the amazing thing!' Eleanor exclaimed. 'It must be something about the air around here, but when I was sure I would be awake half the night I went out like a light.'

Naylor and Lewis were waiting for them, and as Romillie, avoiding Naylor's glance, looked at Lewis, so she saw the way his eyes, his whole face, lit up when he saw her mother. She knew then that Lewis Selby was in love with her parent.

'Good morning, Romillie,' Naylor greeted her, every bit as if he had forgotten their five-thirty meeting.

'Good morning,' she replied, and made herself look at him. While she was not sure that she did not go a bit pink, his expression told her nothing.

They opted to eat in the big old kitchen, now streamlined, the two men taking over the role of cooks. Romillie was not hungry; her insides were too churned up to think of food. But rather than give anyone cause to comment if she did not eat a morsel, she did her best with scrambled egg and toast.

She was not feeling at all talkative; she had far too much on

her mind for that—not least the fact that somehow, catching her
entirely unaware or she would have done something about it,
she had grown to love Naylor. Had, in fact, fallen head over
heels in love with him.

Thankfully the fact that she contributed little to the mealtime
conversation was not noticed, Naylor keeping the conversation
flowing while he explained, in response to Eleanor's question
of where might be a good place to take out a sketchpad, some
of the best views around.

Last night's downpour had given way to a brilliantly sunny
morning, so that, after they'd all lent a hand clearing away
the breakfast dishes and generally tidying up, Lewis suggested he might walk with Eleanor if she wished to do some
sketching.

'It won't be boring for you?' Eleanor asked him, having no
clue, apparently, of his feelings for her.

'I might borrow a sketchpad myself,' he replied.

'You sketch?'

'Badly,' Lewis laughed—and while Lewis and her mother
chatted away on the subject Romillie looked from them. It
seemed that she could not now prevent herself from looking at
Naylor for more than a few minutes at a time. Finding she was
looking straight into his eyes, she had an unnerving feeling he
had been watching her.

'Are you going sketching too?' he asked smoothly.

'I'm—not sure,' she replied, but knew that, with this weekend being about her mother and Lewis spending some time
together, she would not be. 'I'll—er—see you later,' she said
on a gulp of sudden panic, and got out of there.

She knew that had been a stupid thing to do before she was
halfway up the stairs. The trouble was her head was a quagmire
of racing thoughts and she had never felt so thoroughly mixed
up. It was no wonder to her, then, that she had gone sleepwalking. The only wonder, as she reached her room, was that with

so much churning around in her head she hadn't broken out into a sleep 'run' to get away from it all.

Her mother came to her room a half-hour later, saying that she and Lewis would be off shortly, and when Romillie said she would not be going with her and Lewis on their sketching expedition, she replied, 'You'll be all right with Naylor.' Her way, Romillie knew, of saying that she approved of him.

'Have a good sketch,' Romillie bade her brightly—and as her parent went had never felt so down.

She stayed in her room for the next hour, reasoning that, this being Naylor's home, there were obviously things he usually liked to do on a Saturday morning. But in truth she was afraid that, as she had seen love for her mother in Lewis's eyes, so Naylor, with that astute mind and direct look, might see her love for him reflected in her eyes.

Restlessly she paced the floor. She wanted to go home, but could not see how she could. Naylor would be glad to see the back of her, she didn't doubt. Who wouldn't? He was a very private person but, because he had caught her sleepwalking, he had felt obliged to sleep with his bedroom door open.

Oh, grief, he must be looking forward to their departure tomorrow with everything he had! Friendship with Lewis or no, it would be the last time he invited Romillie Fairfax to Oaklands. There was no—

Her thoughts were suddenly halted when someone came and knocked on her door. Startled, her gaze shot to the door. It was Naylor; she knew that it was.

For all of two seconds she was transfixed. No way was she going to answer it. But that was ridiculous! Naylor knew she was there. To answer his knock was the least courtesy she owed him.

Swallowing hard, she went to the door, but had to take a steadying breath before she could open it. Naylor stood there, tall, seeming to fill the doorway. His eyes searched her face as she tried to hide any anxiety he might see in her eyes. 'You're trying to avoid me?' he asked.

Romillie loved him too much for anything other than honesty. 'Yes,' she admitted, 'I am.'

'Something I've done?' he enquired easily.

And Romillie knew then that, as honest as she wanted to be with him, she could not possibly confess that she had fallen in love with him. Though she felt totally ridiculous as, honestly, she blurted out, 'My feet were dirty!' He did not so much as blink. 'Oh, Naylor,' she wailed, 'I went sleepwalking in the night, didn't I?'

'Do you—often?' he enquired, his striking blue eyes steady on her face.

Romillie sensed he was feeling put out that she had not warned him. 'I haven't done it in ages,' she defended.

'How long since?' he wanted to know.

'Not since I was a child—well, with a few exceptions,' she qualified. The last time had been when she had been on the brink of going to university. 'But it only happens when I get anxious or stressed.'

His expression tightened the merest fraction. But his tone was mild, when he questioned, 'You were anxious about being here?'

'No! No, not that!' she quickly assured him. 'Er—do you want to come in?' she offered. It was after all his house, and it did not seem to be quite the thing to be apologising for sleepwalking while keeping him standing in the doorway.

He answered by stepping into her room. He indicated one of the two lovely blue padded chairs. She went and seated herself in one; he took the other. 'You're comfortable here?'

'Who wouldn't be? Your home is a delight, Naylor!'

She didn't know what she expected him to say in reply to that. But her hope that they had finished with the subject of her night time perambulations was a vain hope, she found. And she just knew that he wasn't finished with the subject yet, and that he wanted to know much more than she had told him, when, leaning back in his chair, he casually commented, 'You said you had a bit of an upset yesterday. I think it was larger than just a "bit" of an upset, wasn't it, Romillie?'

She hesitated. 'You—um—you could say that,' she agreed, but had no intention of saying anything more.

Naylor stared at her, observing that hint of stubbornness that was there in the stiff way in which she sat. 'Want to tell me about it?' he invited.

'No!' she replied bluntly. But, because that sounded so terribly curt, 'I'm sorry. I'm sorry if you're—um—cross with me. Sorry that I walked in my sleep—'

'Hold it right there!' he cut in. 'I'm not cross or annoyed with you. You couldn't help—'

'How did you find out?' she butted in, the question only just dawning on her. And, fearfully, in case her subconscious had known of her love before she had, and had led her to go to find him, 'I didn't come into your room, did I?' she asked, wide-eyed and not a little panicky, remembering—or not remembering—unpacking her suitcase that other time; she could have done anything!

'I hadn't gone to bed,' he assured her. 'Everyone else was tucked up for the night, or so I thought. I was in the hall, about to lock up, when I saw you coming down the stairs.'

Belatedly she recalled her grubby feet, which indicated she had been outside and not checking out the rooms. 'I'm sorry if I alarmed you.'

'I was more concerned than alarmed,' Naylor said, smiling encouragingly. 'I realised what was happening when you looked straight through me and headed outside.'

'I wonder where I went?'

'I went with you. You didn't go far. While I was still trying to work out if I should wake you or leave you be, you took a walk around your car, as if to assure yourself that it was still there, and headed back indoors again.'

'I'm sorry,' she apologised again, and found she was telling him, 'I'm thinking about selling it.'

'It must have been on your mind,' he suggested. And asked, 'What model are you thinking of replacing it with?'

'I'm not,' she replied without thinking, and was about to cover that by inventing that now her mother no longer drove they did not really need a car—which she knew they did if she were to continue to go home in her lunch hour—when the most devastating thought struck her. 'Did I have any clothes on?' she gasped in an appalled rush.

'Were you fully dressed—except for shoes—you mean?'

She shook her head. 'Once, one hot summer, I woke up and found my pyjamas on the floor,' she explained faintly. 'I just wondered what—or if—I was wearing...'

'Relax, little Rom,' he teased. 'I've seen you in far less.' For a moment she wasn't with him. Then she recalled how she had walked into the studio and seen him studying that nude sketch of her. 'You blush so delightfully,' he murmured, and, getting to his feet, 'Come on,' he said decisively, 'we'll take a walk around.' That seemed such a very good idea that Romillie got up from her chair too. Though suddenly her heart was racing because, 'Try not to worry,' Naylor instructed and, coming up close, he looked down into her wide brown eyes. 'It will all come right,' he promised.

She didn't know how, but, 'I'm sure you're right,' she agreed. And did not know quite where she was when, 'You look like a young lady who could seriously do with a hug,' he said, and, taking a step closer, he drew her into his arms.

She knew, she knew full well, that she should have done something. Anything but what she did do. But with the feel of his strong arms holding her safe, the temptation was too much. She leaned against him and rested her head on his chest and placed her arms around him. For a short while she seemed to find peace of mind.

Romillie came to her senses when she felt what was a brotherly type of kiss to the top of her head. She pulled away. Her feelings for him were very wide of sisterly.

She took a small step back, and as his arms fell away wished with all that she had that she had not. She wanted those strong arms about her again. She wanted to speak, wanted to say something, but as they stood there, close together still, she did not trust that her voice would come out sounding anything but a croak.

She looked up into unsmiling eyes, into his unsmiling expression. But as Naylor looked down at her, all at once he smiled. And there was nothing whatsoever similarly affected about him, nothing whatsoever croaky in his voice, when he informed her, 'This isn't getting the potatoes peeled.'

She laughed. She loved him. They went from her room and down the stairs and out into glorious sunshine. For the moment just the fact of being with him making her feel happier than she had ever been.

They walked down the oak-tree-lined drive and through the iron-scrolled gates at the bottom. And, in what for her was wonderful companionship, they walked along the road she had driven up the previous evening.

After a while they turned into a lane. It was quite a long lane, but well worth the walk because there at the end was the most lovely view of gently rolling land, of hills in the near distance, and in between, at the very bottom of a steep incline, nestled a small stream that was partly hidden by overhanging willows.

'It's enchanting,' she murmured softly, and went down with Naylor to stand beneath one huge willow and watch the rippling stream. Never had she felt in such complete harmony with him. It was a magical moment.

'I thought you might like this spot,' Naylor commented softly.

Romillie was silent, and appreciative, for long minutes. 'Did you tell my mother about this lovely place?' she asked, thinking that her mother's artist's eyes would love everything about it.

'It is rather special, isn't it?' he commented. 'I'll show Eleanor the next time you come.'

It *was* a special place, and Romillie's heart was filled with love for him. Then what he had just said penetrated. 'You're going to ask us again?' she exclaimed, turning to him.

'If you behave yourself this time,' he replied, but she knew there was a smile in his voice.

She was inwardly smiling too as she said lightly, 'I rather thought, after last night's activities, that I'd blown it for a future invitation.'

'Which just shows you how little you know,' he answered drolly. But he was deadly serious when he asked, 'So what was it all about, Romillie?'

She did not pretend to misunderstand him, though heartily wished she had not brought up her 'last night's activities'. 'I'd rather not talk about it,' she replied as lightly as she could.

Tough! Naylor had decided. 'Davidson?' he enquired. 'Is he behaving himself?'

'He's getting on my nerves, actually,' she confessed without meaning to.

'He's bothering you?'

'I—um—don't seem able to get through to him that when I say it's over, I mean just that.'

'Want me to handle it?'

Romillie looked up at him in astonishment. 'You?' she asked—nobody had ever 'taken up cudgels' on her behalf before! But, on thinking about it, she decided she'd had just about enough of Naylor's 'brotherly' sentiments. Though of course it wasn't his fault that he only saw her in a 'little sister' light. She was beginning to rue that she had ever told him of her virginity—he'd been like this ever since then. Not that he had been lover-like before! 'I'll handle it myself!' she said shortly.

'You do know there's a law against sexual harassment in the workplace?' Naylor questioned.

'I'll bear that in mind.'

There was silence for a while. But, when she thought Naylor was using it to drink in the view after a week of being city-bound, 'So Davidson is only part of the reason for you being upset?' he prodded. Honestly! 'You said *"we"* had a bit of an upset. So whatever upset you, upset your mother too.' Romillie had a grumpy feeling it would be wise to watch every word with this man—he seemed to miss very little. 'And I've an idea,' he went on, 'that you wouldn't let Eleanor know you are having problems with Davidson.' He paused, and then asked, 'So who else has been upsetting you?'

'All this because you caught me taking a stroll at lights-out!' Romillie erupted—and was at once ashamed of herself. She was under his roof, under his protection in a way. She supposed he had a right to question what had so disturbed her that her sleepwalking habit had resurrected itself. 'I'm sorry,' she apologised straight away. 'I'm being unfair.'

'You might feel better if you talked it out of your system.'

'I doubt it.'

'So you're not ready to discuss it?'

'It's—so—so—ugly.' The words were dragged from her.

'I suppose, since Eleanor seems to be involved, that I could ask her.'

'Don't you dare!' Romillie flew, enraged at the very suggestion. 'She—' She broke off, instantly ashamed again. 'I'm sorry,' she apologised. 'It's just, she's been through enough. I don't want her upset.'

'You haven't told her you've started sleepwalking again?'

'No, and you mustn't either. In any case, I'm sure it isn't going to happen again.' Naylor looked sceptical, and she felt she had to explain a little. 'It was just that yesterday was, well, a bit—um—traumatic.'

'You can't possibly leave it there,' he stated, when it became obvious that she had nothing more to say on the subject.

Romillie *would* have left it there. But then she looked at him, and loved him, and needing to say something, anything to get her on a more even keel, found she was revealing, 'My father paid us a visit yesterday. I—er…That is, he visited my mother, but I came home early and he was still there…' My stars, was he! Thank God she *had* come home early.

'He was—pestering Eleanor?' Naylor questioned quietly.

'He wants her to sell the house.'

'Presumably to realise the cash for his half?'

'The house isn't his. It never was. It belonged to my grand-father, my mother's father.'

Naylor took that in in a moment. 'I hope your mother didn't agree to anything so rash?'

'She couldn't,' Romillie answered. 'My father is no good with money, which I think is why my grandfather left the house to my mother, but in trust for me.'

'So it can't be sold, even if Eleanor was agreeable to his demand,' Naylor summed up, and suggested, 'I don't suppose that went down very well?'

'My father's broke again.' Romillie did her best to defend him.

'Your mother naturally gave him some money,' Naylor commented shrewdly.

'All we had,' Romillie replied, quite without thinking.

'Hence you thinking of selling your car.'

Whoa! 'You're much too sharp for me!' she exclaimed, discovering that being in love did not stop you from feeling scratchy.

'So he's now flush, and you and Eleanor are the ones who are broke,' Naylor summarised.

'Look, why can't we just enjoy the view?' Romillie erupted. 'I'd just like to forget all about yesterday!'

'That won't make it go away,' he said gently. Oh, that tone—it was so weakening. 'So your father went on his way, solvent, but without the promise of more.'

'That about sums it up,' she said flatly.

'He was not a happy man?'

'Don't remind me!' she exclaimed with a shudder—and felt Naylor still.

She turned with a pretence of looking at the view on the other side of the stream, but Naylor's hands came to her arms, firm, steady, and turned her to face him. 'He—wasn't—violent?' he asked sternly.

Romillie looked down, wanting to lie. But Naylor let go one hand to place it under her chin, making her look at him—and she found the utmost difficulty in hiding the truth from him.

'I told you it was ugly,' she answered shakily. 'I... Fortunately, I arrived home before—things could get even nastier than they were.'

'You prevented him from assaulting your mother?'

'You—could say that.'

Naylor, his expression grim, took that on board. Then, his voice steely quiet, 'And what about you, Romillie? Did he let you get away with that?'

But, having relived the whole ghastly episode, Romillie shook her head. 'He was still shouting and bellowing, but folded completely and slammed out when I threatened that if he laid a finger on either of us he'd be spending the weekend in the police cells.'

On impulse, it seemed, Naylor just had to bend and place a gentle kiss on her lips, and, while her heartbeat went into overdrive, 'Good for you,' he said quietly. She imagined that his grip on her arm tightened, but knew it for imagination only when he let go his hold and took a step back. 'So you now intend to sell your car?'

'Well, it's my mother's car, actually, but she doesn't drive any more. And prior to my father's visit she was doing so well I could probably have not returned home at lunchtime and could have done without a car too. But... Anyway, it's not all doom and gloom,' she went on, forcing a bright note. 'I've a trust fund from my grandfather that I come into when I'm twenty-five. I'll probably be able to borrow from that.' Fat chance!

'Did they let you have some of it the last time you asked?' Naylor enquired perceptively.

'Oh—shut up!' she exploded—and suddenly they were both laughing. They looked into each other's eyes, and she loved him so just then that she almost told him.

'Romillie!' He said her name, but, remembering how she had read Lewis's love for her mother in his eyes, Romillie abruptly turned away.

They were on the way back to the house, talking of anything other than the subjects that had triggered her sleepwalking when Romillie truly began to enjoy her visit to Naylor and his home. She never, ever wanted to refer to Jeff Davidson, money—or their lack of it—or her father again. She wanted to forget everything about that this weekend. She wanted to put it all behind her. Thanks to Naylor, she was certainly feeling better able to cope than she had.

They were on the drive leading up to the house when she felt, however, that she must refer to it just one more time. 'You won't say anything to Lewis about any of what I've told you, will you?' she asked Naylor.

He looked down at her as they continued walking. 'You don't think it would be helpful to him to know?'

Romillie halted, and Naylor stopped too. She looked up at him, realising that if her mother was out of sorts—and who could blame her?—it might help Lewis to know some of what might lie behind it. But, 'Please, Naylor,' Romillie insisted. 'My mother would be upset if she knew I'd said anything at all to you. She would hate it if Lewis knew too.'

'Have neither of your parents any idea of the emotional battering they've put *you* through?' Naylor grated.

'This isn't about me!' Romillie flew. 'My mother has her own trauma to deal with.'

'So I'm not to tell her that her beautiful daughter has started to sleepwalk again, and I'm to not tell Lewis, my very good friend, who might be aided by such information, that the woman he—cares—for had a particularly rough time yesterday?'

Romillie was stuck on the word beautiful. Did Naylor think her beautiful? 'That's right!' she said stiffly.

'You're angry with me?' Naylor asked, relenting, his mouth picking up at the corners.

She wanted to laugh, but stubbornly wouldn't. 'You are one very annoying male,' she told him.

'Why?' he wanted to know.

'Because—because, oh, I don't know what it is about you, but you have me telling you things I'd have said I wouldn't dream of telling a soul.'

Naylor considered that. 'Hmm! It could be that I'm on the way to being your best friend.'

She laughed. She had to. 'Oh, you!' she exclaimed lamely.

'Want to kiss and make up?'

Romillie was fast realising that, so great was the hold this man had over her, she could not stay angry with him for more than about ten seconds at a time. On impulse she stretched up and kissed him. He stilled and she wanted more—but made herself pull back.

That Saturday turned out to be one of the best days Romillie could remember. Both her mother and Lewis seemed to be glowing when they returned from their sketching expedition. They had a salad lunch and spent the afternoon relaxing, and went out for dinner in the evening.

By some unspoken consent Romillie sat up front with Naylor to and from the restaurant. She felt dreamy and contented on their return back to Oaklands, and never wanted the ride to end.

But all too soon they were turning into the oak-tree-lined drive. They went indoors, where Naylor suggested a nightcap. Eleanor declined.

'It's been a lovely day, but all that fresh air seems to have got to me. I think I'll go up, if no one minds.'

'I'll come too,' Romillie said with a smile. She sorely wanted to stay down with Naylor, but she must not be greedy. She would see him again tomorrow.

Not that he seemed at all put out. 'Sleep tight,' he bade her. He kissed her and smiled into her eyes—and she was all at sixes and sevens.

'Goodnight,' she said generally, hoping no one else had picked up the husky note in that one word. Naylor's 'Sleep tight', she knew, was his way of saying try not to worry and get some rest. His kiss meant nothing. It had been light, and not for her benefit but because her mother was there.

They were halfway up the staircase, Naylor and Lewis heading for the drawing room, when her mother stated, 'You're—fond of him, aren't you, darling?'

Romillie did not pretend not to know who she was meaning. 'Does it show?' she asked, panic stricken.

'Only to me.'

Romillie relaxed. 'He's—different,' she managed, her panic subsiding.

'They both are,' her mother replied, and, with an imp of mischief that had long since been absent, 'Quite obviously we've been mixing in the wrong company.'

Romillie laughed. It was so good to see her mother like this. Coming here this weekend had done her nothing but good.

Once in her room and alone, Romillie made herself think only of pleasant things. She would 'sleep tight'; she would not go on any more 'moonlight saunters'.

She got into bed, concentrating only on her pleasant day. Monday, and being plagued by Jeff Davidson, was something she would handle on Monday, not now. Monday, and bills to be paid with money they no longer had, was something she would have to worry about then. As for her father—she would find some way of seeking legal advice; though off-hand she could not think of anyone who would advise her for free.

Stop it, stop it! Think pleasant thoughts. Naylor. He could annoy her, make her scratchy, but, oh, how she loved him. 'It could be that I'm on the way to being your best friend,' he'd said. She fell asleep knowing that he had been joking, but knowing that she would love to have him as her best friend.

She slept soundly that night—or thought she did. Unsure, the first thing she did on waking was to take a look at her feet. Not a scrap of dirt on them. She checked her white mule-type slippers, but they were pristine, with no evidence that they had been anywhere outside of her room.

Presentable feet did not mean to say that she had not gone for a stroll around the house, though. Feeling disquieted, she checked the time. Still far too early to get up, but she knew she would not go back to sleep again.

Romillie was aware by then that the plumbing was first class, and her shower next to silent. It was still early, though, when showered, dressed and ready for the day, she sat in the window seat. Summer was at its height, and it was quite daylight, had been for some while, as she sat and drank in the lovely grounds of Naylor's home.

A half an hour later and she started to grow restless, her brain fidgeting with thoughts of how she had started to sleepwalk again. Another quick check of the time and she realised that her mother was probably up and dressed too by now.

Silently Romillie left her room. She closed her door with barely a whisper of sound. But as she went carefully along the landing—mindful of the chance of stepping on a creaky floorboard—she suddenly spotted that Naylor's bedroom door was ajar! She came to an abrupt halt.

She froze, listening. She heard not a sound. Naylor was not up and about, and she was pretty sure his door was open solely for her benefit. Oh, the dear man! He must be praying for this weekend to be over so he could get some rest. Despite what he had said yesterday, she knew he would not be inviting her to Oaklands ever again. Not that his invitation this weekend had been for her benefit anyway. He had witnessed the dreadful time his friend had been through, and knew Lewis was keen on her mother, who had been through her own dreadful time. It was his way of trying to help.

Endeavouring to remember where that creaky floorboard of yesterday was, Romillie had just successfully circumnavigated it, and had stretched out a careful hand to noiselessly close Naylor's door, when, totally unexpectedly, it was pulled wide—and she was yanked inside.

'Caught you, my lovely!' Naylor cried wickedly, like some pirate of old.

Romillie, who did not go in for giggling—just had to giggle. 'You dastardly cad!' she managed, absently observing that he was shirt and trouser-clad.

But suddenly, as they looked at each other, some mutual chemistry seemed to kick in, and, 'Oh, Romillie,' Naylor groaned, and the next she knew she was in his arms and his head was nearing hers.

There was absolutely no thought in her head not to meet him halfway. Pliant in his arms, it was wonderful to feel his mouth over hers in a breathtaking kiss.

'Naylor,' she murmured, his name leaving her involuntarily.

'You object?' he asked, his eyes searching hers.

She stretched up and kissed him. 'Do I look as if I'm objecting?' she asked softly.

And had her reward when, long and lingeringly, he kissed her again. Her heart was racing when he pulled back and looked down into her eyes. She made herself remember that he must not see her love for him. And, while she never wanted to leave his arms, and was sure a few snatched kisses would not hurt, she tried hard for something coherent and at the same time unrevealing to say.

'I didn't—did I?' she asked, which even to her own ears sounded far from coherent.

But, as ever sharp and clear thinking—the same of which could not be said of her—Naylor seemed to be able to unravel her question. 'You didn't,' he answered.

She gave a relieved sigh, loving the feel of his strong arms around her. 'Thank goodness for that,' she replied, only then realising how much the fear of again walking in her sleep had bothered her. 'Ooh—were you on guard all night?' she asked, starting to feel extremely guilty. 'Have you slept at all?'

'I'm a light sleeper,' he said, and, smiling down at her, 'Do you think you could shut up for a minute?'

And before she could formulate any reply Naylor was showing her he had another purpose for her mouth, when his head came down again and he claimed her lips with his.

Romillie had no thought to deny him. Her arms went around him, holding him close. She loved him and felt starved of him. She returned his kisses, a fire starting to burn in her, making her want more and yet more.

Coherent thought seemed a thing of the past when Naylor drew back and again looked into her eyes. She strove hard for clear thought, though, as some hint of sense, of reason, strove to get through to her.

'Er...' she said, and faltered before she started.

'What—er?' Naylor asked softly, a gentle smile for her on his mouth, in his eyes.

Romillie swallowed hard. 'Er—it just occurred to me,' she brought out from an unthought nowhere, 'that—um—for platonic sort of—friends, we're doing an awful lot of kissing.'

His smile became a grin. 'Want to go for broke?'

She was not at all sure what he meant by that, but settled for a non-committal answer. 'At this hour?'

Naylor laughed out loud. 'Oh, my—have you a lot to learn, Miss Fairfax.'

Teach me! Teach me! 'There's no answer to that,' she laughed in response, but supposed she gave him her answer in that she stretched up and kissed him.

Naylor did not neglect her answer, but returned her kiss with an increasing warmth, and all at once she was up in his arms and he was carrying her over to his bed.

'Er...' she murmured, when Naylor set her down on the mattress and came and lay down beside her.

'Don't worry,' he reassured her, propping himself up on an elbow and looking down on her. 'We're not going to go too far. I just thought it would be—um—educational for you to lie on a bed with a wanting male.'

Romillie stared up at him, startled, uncertain which to go for first. She tried both. 'This is furthering my education!' she exclaimed. And, hot on the heels of that, 'You want me?'

'Right at this moment I'm drawing on all my reserves of strength to not take hold of you and ravish you till you beg for mercy,' he replied lightly—and she could not tell whether he was serious or whether he wasn't.

'I take it from that that I'm not going to be ravished today,' she said, laughing inside, loving inside, feeling in no way threatened, and just then his to do with what he would.

All-seeing striking blue eyes devoured her. 'We could make a start, I suppose,' he murmured, and bent his head and kissed her long and hungrily. But then suddenly he pulled back and sat up. 'I think,' he said, in a voice a little thick in his throat, 'that it might be an idea if you went now.'

Romillie's mouth fell open and she too sat up. 'You *do* want me!' she exclaimed.

Naylor stared back at her unsmiling. 'So I'm not as bright as I thought I was.'

'Never!' she tried to tease.

'Cut that out or I really will ravish you,' he threatened.

'Why aren't you as bright...?'

'I thought, when I heard you outside my door, to start the day on a fun note—hopefully make you laugh before breakfast. I like to hear you laugh,' he threw in. 'Only I must have overlooked that—despite your lack of experience—you are a beautiful and most desirable woman.'

Romillie was still staring at him open-mouthed. She knew she should get up off his bed and leave. But she did not want to. She wanted to savour every moment of this closeness with him. Closeness which instinct was telling her would never come again.

'So that's it, is it? My education's over?'

'You're asking for trouble,' he warned.

Yes, please. 'I'd better go, then.'

'I'll see you later.'

She laughed. Again she felt that urge to tell him that she loved him, but she knew the folly of that. She made to get up from the bed, but hesitated. 'Want to shake hands?' she asked impishly.

He laughed, which was what she was after. 'Come here,' he muttered, and took her face between his two hands and gently kissed her. It was a wonderful kiss, and she just had to hold him, knowing that any second now he would pull back and wish her *adieu*. Only just then they both heard a sound over by the wide open door.

Shooting a jerky glance over to it, Romillie saw her mother standing there. She had obviously been on her way past when she had noticed her daughter in the room. Romillie realised she could not have missed seeing them kissing in what must look like a loving embrace. She saw her mother smile contentedly before she swiftly went on her way.

'Oh, grief!' Romillie exclaimed. Without question Naylor had seen her mother standing there too. Hastily Romillie let go of him, only then realising that she had not been merely holding him but had unthinkingly put her arms around him. She sought for something bright to say, but in the absence of anything sparkling coming to her found a touch of humour to help her get out of there. 'You do know, I hope, that now my mother has seen me in bed with you that you're going to have to marry me?' she informed him.

Naylor stared at her, stunned, and she guessed that her solemnly delivered comment must have shaken him to the core. And knew it when he sharply reprimanded, 'Don't say that— even in jest!'

And, strangely, that hurt. 'Pardon me for breathing!' she snapped, but saw him lighten up, a smile beginning as he took on board that she had not been serious, and recalled that she was no more marriage-minded than he was. Romillie edged over the bed. 'Saw the whites of your eyes then, Cardell, didn't I?' she jibed.

He made a grab for her. She squealed—and got out of there.

But back in her room it suddenly wasn't so funny. She had told him, in jest certainly, that he would have to marry her. But not so very long ago such words to any man would have been utterly distasteful to her. Yet just now, when she had said them to Naylor, they had not felt distasteful at all.

Most perturbingly, causing her to collapse into the nearest chair, Romillie realised that her views and feelings about marriage were undergoing something of a very serious change!

# CHAPTER SIX

THEIR weekend at Oaklands was with Romillie all through the hours of Sunday night, her thoughts mainly of Naylor. After their 'fun' start to the morning they had both been a little aloof with each other. She because she did not want him to think she placed the smallest importance to the way they had kissed and held each other. He, she guessed, because he was sorely regretting that he 'liked to hear her laugh'.

He had lightly kissed her goodbye, true, but that had been because her mother was there. Romillie had known, as she resurrected her phoney smile to bid him goodbye, that goodbye it was. A steely glint had entered his eyes, as if he did not care for her phoney smile, but she'd ignored it, thanked him prettily for his hospitality—and had known that that was it. She would never see Oaklands again, and if he had anything to do with it she would never see him again either.

She was awake early on Monday morning and heard sounds that told her her mother could not sleep either and was already on the move. Putting from her thoughts of having to go to work and deal with Jeff Davidson, Romillie showered and dressed and went downstairs to find her mother sitting staring into space.

'You look worried?' Romillie commented.

'I've one or two things on my mind.'

'Dad?' Romillie guessed. 'You're worried he might turn up again? I can stay home from work if—'

'I've worried enough about him,' Eleanor butted in, and, finding a smile, 'At about three o'clock this morning I reached decision time.' And, apologetically going on, 'I've taken just about enough from that man. I'm sorry, Rom, but if you've no objection I've decided I'm going to do what you said. The next time he shows up and starts behaving in the way he did last Friday, I'm going to see a solicitor and see about forbidding him from coming anywhere near. And before you start to worry about how we are going to pay for such legal services, I thought, if you're agreeable, we might sell the car. We'll need some money from somewhere anyway—that boiler isn't going to last through the winter.'

Romillie was amazed. Her mother was an artist, she just wasn't practical, things such as a clapped-out boiler just weren't in her terms of reference. 'Did you sleep at all last night?' Romillie exclaimed.

'I told you I'd one or two things on my mind.'

With her mother being in such a positive frame of mind, Romillie drove to work realising that it looked as though her nightmare fears about her father were about to be dealt with once and for all. Archer Fairfax had a sort of inverted pride in that, while he could create all sorts of mayhem within the home the threat of legal action and anyone knowing about it outside of the home was something he just could not take. It was a wonder to her that they had not thought of such action before. Although up until recently she would have said her mother was not strong enough to go through with it.

All of which made Romillie realise that things were most definitely picking up! She had pondered on the best way to broach the subject of selling the car; Romillie now knew that she did not have to ponder any more. Her mother, so much stronger now, had taken on board that their bills had to be paid, and had reached the same conclusion for herself—the car would have to go.

Which, Romillie saw as she parked at the surgery, left her with only one problem to deal with. Jeff Davidson. Naylor and her love for him she had to leave—she was never going to be able to resolve that one.

Though something Naylor had said to her on Saturday was there in her head when at his earliest opportunity Jeff Davidson sought her out.

'I have decided,' she began coldly before he could do more than place a familiar hand on her shoulder, 'that unless you stop harassing me, I shall report you to the senior partner.'

'I'm not harassing!' he denied, as though amazed. 'You...'

Romillie looked pointedly at his hand on her shoulder. Reluctantly he removed it. But, in case he still had not got it, 'You'll agree, I'm sure, that you would not want the names of dental surgeons East and Davidson cited in the papers for sexual harassment in the workplace.'

*He went!* All that he had put her through—and it had been *that* simple! She could hardly believe it. Jeff Davidson's behaviour had been a kind of bullying, and bullies had to be stood up to—that she was feeling more weak at the knees than brave afterwards was well worth it. Thank you, Naylor. Stop! She was on the Naylor circuit again, though it was a truth that he was very seldom from her mind.

Romillie went home at lunchtime and found her mother still in positive frame of mind. She went back to work still hardly believing that she had heard the last from Jeff Davidson, yet she heard not another peep out of him that day that was not work-related.

With Naylor in her head she drove home after work and discovered yet another matter to be cheered about. 'We don't have to sell the car!' her mother greeted her.

'Some long-lost relative we never knew about has left us a fortune?'

Eleanor shook her head. 'I've had a visitor.'

'Lewis?'

'Someone I met at that art gallery function we went to.' And, while Romillie recalled the event, some weeks ago now, and recalled too the many friends her mother had renewed her acquaintanceship with, 'I've sold a couple of pieces of my work!' Eleanor exclaimed.

'You've sold a couple of paintings!' Romillie was astonished. It had been years since her mother had sold any of her work. That was to say, she had not done any work for so long she'd had very little to sell. 'Which ones?' she asked, feeling so happy for her. The recent ones of the garden were a start, but…

'I sold that one I did years ago—the one in the hall.'

'It was a favourite!'

'I know, but he so admired it and offered such a brilliant price it seemed to be the answer to all my prayers.' She smiled as she added, 'I thought it about time I got realistic—I sold him another more recent small one as well.'

That would be one of the ones of the corner of the garden, Romillie guessed. But with her mother being so 'up' she had to be happy and did not want to spoil her mood by asking questions that might make her doubtful that she had done the right thing and might dim her happiness. As it was her mother's confidence was soaring that after such a long lay-off someone had wanted to purchase a more recent work too.

Romillie knew she would miss that lovely picture in the hall, but supposed she had better be realistic too. They did need the money. But that her mother's old acquaintance had paid for the paintings in cash seemed a little strange, because it was no small amount. Although on recalling a few of the 'arty'—even a touch weird—types at the gallery that night, perhaps it wasn't so strange.

In any event, with their savings jar now full to overflowing,

Romillie could hardly credit that all the problems that on Friday night had seemed so totally insurmountable were so satisfactorily resolved.

The next two days dragged by; loving Naylor and being apart from him seemed to have slowed down time. But she drove home from work on Thursday—Jeff Davidson still keeping his distance—feeling quite light-headed that for once it seemed neither she nor her mother had anything to worry about.

It was around midnight, though, as she lay in bed aching to be near Naylor, that the telephone rang—and she discovered she had been a bit previous in her belief that they had nothing more to worry about.

For a brief while she considered not answering it. Since no one rang them at this hour it was only going to be a wrong number anyway. But she was awake, and if her mother was sound away there was little point in her being disturbed by the constant ringing.

Hastening down the stairs, Romillie picked up the phone and said, 'Hello,' fully expecting to be asked if she were the George Hotel, their most frequent misdial.

'Romillie.' It was Naylor! Her heart threatened to leap out of her body. Her lips formed his name, but she was so shaken to hear him so unexpectedly that no sound came. But Naylor was not waiting, but quietly, calmly, he was relating, 'Lewis is in hospital.' In an instant her thoughts went to the man she only then realised she had become quite fond of.

'What's wrong?' she asked quickly, her thought flying from ill, to accident, and on to her mother, whom she felt must hold Lewis in some quite high regard.

'They suspect a heart attack. He's being assessed now.' And, while Romillie was starting to feel fearful, 'I apologise for ringing you at this hour, but I believe Eleanor cares for him and would want to know.'

'Yes, of course,' Romillie replied, and, as she began to get her head back together, 'Which hospital?' she asked.

Naylor told her, adding, 'I'm there now.'

'Thank you for letting me know. I'll tell my mother.'

There was a pause at the other end. Then Naylor's voice again as he bade her a crisp, 'Goodnight!'

Romillie put down her phone and went straight to her mother's room. 'Are you asleep?' she whispered into the darkness.

Her mother sat up, switching on her bedside light as she did so. 'Did I hear the phone?'

'Naylor's just rung.' And, no way to dress it up, 'Lewis has had a suspect heart attack.'

'Lewis…' Eleanor gasped, her colour draining.

'It isn't certain,' Romillie said quickly. 'But he's in hospital being assessed.'

From that moment on, Romillie began to see a woman she had never seen before, a strong and decisive woman, the woman her mother must have been before her spirit had been stamped on and left for dead.

'Ring Naylor back,' she requested firmly, flinging the bedcover away and getting out of bed. 'Ask him which hospital and—'

'He told me which hospital.'

'Good.' Her mother was already at her chest of drawers, pulling out fresh underwear. 'Let me have the car keys, there's a love. You'll be able to make your way to work tomorrow without it if I'm not back?' she thought to enquire.

Her mother hadn't driven in years! The fact that she would now, now that the man she obviously *did* care for was in trouble, showed Romillie that she must care for Lewis very, very deeply.

'I'll drive you,' she instantly volunteered, pushing her own worry about Lewis to one side. Neither of them wasted time in arguing the merits of who went and who stayed, or who drove or didn't drive. Within the next fifteen minutes Romillie was steering the car out of the drive.

Fortunately at that time in the morning traffic was not heavy, and with Romillie putting her foot down they made it to the hospital in near record time.

Once again she was amazed at the positive change in her mother. For she it was who led the way to find someone who could tell them where Mr Lewis Selby had been taken. Eleanor it was who very near sprinted off to find him.

Romillie was vaguely aware of ascending in a lift, of going along a corridor—but then suddenly, as they turned about, having gone in the wrong direction, there coming towards them was Naylor.

'How is he?' Eleanor asked the moment she saw him.

'They're still waiting for some blood test results, but on the evidence so far, it appears Lewis had suffered a mild heart attack.'

'Mild?' Eleanor seemed to take heart. 'Can I see him?' she asked, looking around.

Naylor explained that there were medical staff with him at the moment, and escorted them to a small waiting area where, ten minutes later, an efficient-looking head nurse came to tell Naylor he could go in and see Mr Selby again now.

'I'd like to see him too.' Eleanor spoke up before Naylor could make the request for her.

'Are you a relative?' the nurse asked.

'I'm his fiancée,' Eleanor, to Romillie's complete amazement, replied.

'If you'd wait just a moment,' the nurse replied kindly, and beetled off.

'You're engaged to Lewis?' Romillie gasped.

'He asked me to marry him,' her mother replied.

It still wasn't going in. Romillie was still in shock as she asked, 'You said yes?'

Her mother gave a self-conscious smile. 'I just did,' she affirmed.

And suddenly Romillie was beaming. She gave her a kiss. 'Just remember when you tell Lewis you've accepted his proposal that he's in here for a suspected heart condition,' she warned, smiling.

The nurse came back. 'Only one of you,' she said. It went without saying that Eleanor was the one who went to see him.

'Did you know Lewis had asked my mother to marry him?' Romillie asked Naylor as they sat down.

'I could see it coming, though that's one thing he didn't confide in me,' Naylor answered, and, looking into her lovely brown eyes, 'You don't seem to mind too much.'

'They'll be good together,' she replied. 'Since knowing Lewis my mother has become so much stronger. Tonight, when I told her Lewis was in trouble, she was immediately ready to drive herself here. She hasn't driven in years,' Romillie explained, and asked, 'Somebody phoned you to say Lewis had been taken ill?'

'I was with him,' Naylor answered. 'We have something of an important meeting tomorrow. I was at Lewis's home, sorting out the last of the nitty-gritty with him, when I noticed he didn't look well. When he confessed to chest pains along with the sweating and nausea, I thought it time to take action.'

'I'm glad you were with him.'

'So am I.'

'You'll have to attend your meeting without him,' she realised.

'I know the way he wants it to go,' Naylor replied.

'Can you not cancel?' she asked in sudden concern. And, feeling a little foolish suddenly, because it was nothing to do with her, 'I mean—' she glanced at her watch '—it's nearly two in the morning; you'll be feeling rubbishy before you start.' She had another thought. 'Though I suppose you're often out to gone two in the morning and still put in a full day's work the following day.'

Naylor favoured her with a wry look. 'It has been known,' he drawled.

Romillie shut up after that. Better to say nothing than for Naylor to know that her concern for him came from the depth of her feelings for him.

'How are things with you and Davidson?' he asked, and she realised he was trying to keep a lid on his fears for Lewis. 'Is he still hounding you?'

It was an anxious time all round, but Romillie found a smile as she revealed, 'Thanks to you I was able to hit him with your comment about sexual harassment in the workplace. That and a promise to report him to the senior partner seems to have done the trick.'

'He hasn't bothered you since?'

She shook her head. 'No, and it's wonderful.'

A short while later her mother came to find them. 'Lewis is looking much better than I expected, but I'd rather not leave,' she said as Romillie and Naylor stood and went forward to meet her. 'You have work tomorrow,' she addressed her daughter. 'You go home now and I'll phone you either there or at—'

'I'll stay with you,' Romillie said at once. It would never occur to her to leave her there alone.

But that was when she discovered that the transition of her mother from the timid, frightened and downtrodden person she had been into this positive know her own mind woman was complete.

'No,' she said flatly. But, to soften that refusal, 'You've looked after me for long enough, Rom. I know where I'm going now. You go home to bed. You've only a few hours before you have to get up again.'

From protective habit Romillie was reluctant to leave her on her own, and might have protested anyway. But, 'I'll take Romillie home,' Naylor cut in.

Romillie later realised that, when for ages it had been down to her to make whatever decisions had to be made, she must have been in some sort of shock that first her mother and then Naylor appeared to be making decisions for her.

Because Naylor had gone along to check that he could safely leave without worrying unduly about Lewis, and at her mother's determined suggestion that she was quite able to drive herself home tomorrow Romillie found she was handing over the keys to the car. And she and Naylor were out of the hospital and sitting in his car—all before she'd had the chance to get her head around any of it.

'I can't let you do this, Naylor,' she told him bluntly as they left the hospital car park.

'I didn't touch you,' he said.

She smiled in the darkness. 'It's ridiculous,' she said firmly. 'If you take me all the way home you'll hardly see your bed at all tonight.'

'True,' he conceded, but added casually after a moment, 'I can offer you a bed at my place if you like?' And while she was realising he meant his London *pied-à-terre,* and her heart went bumpity-bump at this chance to stay near him, he went on to suggest, 'I shall be looking in on Lewis before I go to the office in the morning. You could come with me and…'

'And from there drive my mother home,' Romillie finished for him. 'That is, if my mother is ready to leave.' It sounded the sensible thing to do, but with her heart hurrying up its beat, she had to admit she was not feeling very sensible just then. 'If you're sure…' she began. But the matter was already settled. In no time Naylor was garaging his car at a modern apartment building.

As apartments went it was not an overlarge one, but since she guessed he preferred to go to his home in the Cotswolds if he possibly could, the apartment as he showed her over so she should get her bearings was more than adequate.

Whichever way the layout had been designed, Romillie soon saw that Naylor had adapted it to the way that suited him, in that the first room on the left, which might have been meant as a dining room or a spare bedroom, was now a sitting room. He had turned the room next to it into an office, with desk, chairs and a computer and other machinery. There were bathroom facilities opposite and a kitchen. And lastly, emphasising to her that it was not his home, but merely a place where he could rest his head if he did not want to make the drive to his preferred Cotswolds home should he have been working or partying late, tucked away was a door to the room she thought must be his bedroom.

'Would you like something to drink?' Naylor enquired.

'No, thank you,' she answered. She felt out on her feet, but her concern was for him. He had been working all day, and working most of the evening by the sound of it. On top of that he had witnessed his close friend suffer the onset of heart failure and had needed to take some rapid action.

'If you're sure,' Naylor commented politely, 'I'll show you where you can sleep,' and did no more than open the door they were standing by. As she had suspected, the tucked-away room was a bedroom.

It was a good-sized bedroom, but obviously all male—down to the pair of shoes that were lodged at the foot of the mahogany gentleman's valet. 'Oh! This is your room!' she exclaimed as it dawned on her that, whatever the original layout, Naylor had thought just one bedroom sufficient.

'Not to worry,' he answered easily. 'My Saturday tidy-up lady will have changed the bedlinen, and I haven't slept here at all this week.'

'That wasn't what I was meaning!' Romillie protested, and, certain by then that he must have turned any second bedroom into an office, making this a one-bedroom-only apartment, 'Where are you going to sleep?'

'No need for you to get uptight,' Naylor replied humorously. 'I'll take the sofa.'

She did not find it funny. 'No, you won't! she contradicted. He was a big man and much more suited to the king-size bed than the sofa in the sitting room. 'I'll take the sofa,' she informed him determinedly, and took a step to go from the room, only to find her way was blocked.

'Look here, Romillie Fairfax,' Naylor began firmly, all sign of humour gone, 'you're tired and I'm tired, but you're the one with the sleepwalking habit.' And, while she stared up at him, startled that he should bring that up, 'The sofa in the sitting room is much too close to the outer door,' he added crisply.

She looked at him, puzzled, and had to confess, 'I'm not with you. I've lost you somewhere.'

He drew a long, patient breath. 'This is a relatively new building,' he enlightened her.

She could see that for herself. 'So?'

'The floors are solid, which means that there aren't any floor-boards here to alert me if you decide to take a turnabout outside.'

'Ah!' The penny dropped. 'You think you'll have more chance of hearing me if I have to pass where you're sleeping, rather than if you're tucked away in the bedroom?'

'Whether you appreciate it or not, you've had a pretty stress-ful time of it of late—one way and another it's been a fairly stressful night too,' he said, when in her view he'd had a much more stressful time of it. 'Truly, Rom,' he said, his tone gentling out, 'I just can't have you trotting around London, naked, in the middle of the night.'

'Nak...' She had half said 'naked' before she recalled telling him of the time she had woken up to find she had taken her clothes off in her sleep.

'Oh, Naylor!' she wailed, half exasperated and half trying not to see his point.

She did not want him to sleep on the sofa, yet he had that look about him that said he was not prepared to yield. He was a big man, and that king-sized bed was much more suited to him than a sofa. And, more, he looked tired. He had admitted he was tired. And he had a very important meeting not too many hours from now.

'Tell you what,' she said, striving hard to keep her sense of balance, striving hard for the same humour he had found, 'if you're as tired as I think you are, and you yourself say you are, then I suppose—if you're that worried—we could—um—share.'

His brow went up. 'Share?' he queried, when she was certain he knew exactly what she was meaning. And, when he noticed the faint trace of pink in her cheeks, 'You really are innocent, aren't you?'

Already she was regretting the suggestion. And yet, if something was not soon resolved, neither of them would get any sleep that night. 'I m-meant in a purely platonic way,' she said in a rush, only then realising that he was taking her suggestion seriously—when she was starting to be uncertain whether she had meant what she had said, or had merely been voicing some way out of this impasse.

He *was* serious, she discovered, when, after a long drawn-out but decisive sort of breath, 'Right,' he said, and in no time flat he had found a casual shirt and a pair of cotton shorts for her to sleep in, and disappeared for ten minutes while she visited the bathroom, changed into her overlarge 'nightclothes' and quickly went back to the bedroom.

Not keen for him to catch a glimpse of her so outrageously clad, Romillie quickly got into bed. She kept to the edge, only then appreciating how very tired she was.

She was already drifting off to sleep when she heard the door open and then felt Naylor get into the bed. In true platonic fashion, he too stayed well over to his side of the bed.

Perhaps it was the wonder that he was so close, the wonderful wonder of it, this superb memory for her to keep, that she felt so totally relaxed, that she fell almost instantly asleep.

Romillie slept for what she thought must be one splendid hour. But she was unused to having a bed partner, and awoke the moment she bumped into him. She turned back on to her side, away from him, and must have nodded off again.

But it could not have been too long afterwards that she awoke again. Only this time, and with a feeling of pure bliss, it was to realise that while she was still on her side, she was more into the middle of the bed now—and that Naylor was there too. She was on her right side, he was on his right side, with an arm across her waist, and they seemed to be lightly moulded together.

She only just held in a sigh of pleasure. Never had she been this close to any man, and this man was the man she was in love with. With Naylor's arm about her she felt safe and secure for one of the few times in her life. With his arm over her there was no way she was going anywhere without him knowing it. She closed her eyes, savouring the joy, loving him so much she felt her heart would burst with it.

She drifted off into a light doze, but surfaced again to find that magically they were still in the same position. Her back was against his chest, her bottom in his lap.

She moved to get even closer—and came wide awake to know that Naylor was awake too and had felt her wriggling, 'Keep still!' he grunted—and she knew she had ruined the magic when his arm dragged away from her and he turned over.

They were now back to back. Naylor put more space between them. She wanted to turn over and hold him as he had held her, but knew that she dared not.

Romillie was awake for some while, but realised she must have drifted off at some point when the next she knew was that daylight had crept into the room. She stirred and, with a jolt, her eyes flew wide. She and Naylor were no longer back to back, but were now lying facing each other, and he was awake too! In fact she found she was looking straight into his striking blue eyes.

Suddenly, as she wondered just how long he had been awake, just lying there watching her, she felt too choked to speak. She felt confused all at once and wanted to say something, anything. But, confused or no, knowing that this moment was never going to come again, there was no way she wanted to leap out of bed and fracture it.

'Good morning,' Naylor greeted her quietly.

'What time is it?' she answered huskily.

'How do you like your eggs?' he asked courteously—and she burst out laughing.

'Oh, Naylor—you'll be the death of me.' He smiled and looked, as he had once said, as if he liked the sound of her laughter. Impulsively, seeming unable to stop herself, she leaned towards him and lightly kissed him. But she drew back, instantly appalled by what she had done. 'Sorry!' she exclaimed urgently. 'That wasn't a very good idea, was it?'

Hating herself that she had spoilt this lovely intimate time with him, she went to rocket from the bed. But, before she had moved more than a few inches, Naylor had caught a hold of her, 'Oh I wouldn't say that,' he murmured, and the next she knew she had her back to the mattress and Naylor was half over her, showing her what a good-morning kiss was really like.

Who could resist? Certainly not her. Naylor broke his kiss, and, staring down at her, looked as though he would kiss her again. But then he seemed to agree with her that perhaps it was not such a very good idea after all. He made to move away. Only this time it was she who held on to him.

Naylor looked down at her, seemed to hesitate, and then, as if her kissable mouth and the invitation her lips freely displayed was just too much, he lowered his head and gently teased those lips apart.

'Oh, Naylor!' she gasped, when he drew back and looked deeply into her melting brown eyes.

He gave a sort of groan, and, as if he could not resist her, kissed her again. Nor did it stop at just one kiss. In an enchanted world, Romillie kissed him in return, holding on to him, never wanting this moment to end.

Gentle hands caressed her back, sensitive fingers finding their way beneath the hem of the shirt she wore. Naylor was similarly attired, but as he was not wearing pyjamas she guessed that he normally slept naked and had only donned a shirt and shorts for her benefit.

Her hand searched their way beneath his shirt, and it was bliss pure and simple to feel the smooth warm skin of his back beneath her touch, her own emotions spiralling out of control at the feel of his hands on her naked skin.

They kissed again, and somehow she was the one lying over him. She looked down at him and felt dizzy with rapture when his hands slipped down to her behind and he pulled her into him.

'Naylor!' she gasped.

'I've alarmed you?' he asked softly.

No, not a bit. But she couldn't tell him, she felt too full to speak, so shook her head. And, as though he was not quite sure what signals she was sending, his hands left her behind—but only to move upwards to her breasts.

She held in a gasp at the wonder of the sensations he was creating in her, but had not the smallest objection to make when he breathed, 'I want to see you.'

She knew he meant that he wanted to see her naked, but she still felt somehow too shy to verbally agree. She went to sit up—and discovered she was somehow sitting astride his body. Nothing seemed to surprise her any more as she stretched out her hand and began to unbutton the shirt he had on, hoping that he would see she was in full agreement with anything he wanted of her.

He smiled. 'Sweetheart,' he murmured, and needed no second invitation. He unbuttoned her shirt and took it from her—and that was when she suffered a most unexpected moment of modesty and held her hands in front of her breasts.

Naylor smiled understandingly, and first removed his own shirt before gently reaching up for her. 'Come here,' he said softly, adjusting their position so that he was half sitting with her, coming closer, their nakedness making electric contact.

They kissed, and Romillie felt as though she was breathlessly drowning. As his arms came around her, she put her arms around him, glorying in the feel of broad manly chest against the full and firm cushion of her bosom.

'Sweet love,' Naylor murmured, and pulled back to look into her flushed face and then down to her pink-tipped exquisite breasts. This time she made no attempt to cover herself from his gaze. 'Oh, my beautiful Romillie,' he breathed, and she adored him.

She stared at him—at his broad chest, his inviting nipples—and again felt that she was drowning, her desire for him shooting up, going out of orbit, when he gently kissed first one hardened tip of her breast and then the other.

Tenderly he kissed her again, and gradually, as his kisses became more ardent, Romillie started to become aware of a change in their lovemaking. Naylor's kisses, while still being giving, were becoming gently demanding too. And that was quite all right as far as she in her utter enchantment was concerned.

She was utterly enraptured by him when he manoeuvred to adjust their positions and lay down with her—her heart thumping to discover she was on her back with Naylor between her thighs.

She panicked slightly, though not enough to want to end it. The time, she knew, had passed when she could have called a halt. But, with the feel of his wanting body so close, she looked up at him, her face burning, as she covered any panic that might make *him* call a halt and asked huskily, teasingly, '*This* is platonic?'

Naylor looked deeply into her eyes. 'If we carry on like this much longer, Miss Fairfax, I really am going to have to consider marrying you,' he replied, and his head came nearer, as if he would kiss her again.

But his words hurt. Cruelly hurt and cut to the heart of her. Because she suddenly became fully aware that she would love to marry him. But at the same time was also fully aware too that there was no way that Naylor Cardell would ever consider to marry her. And his words—never more cruel in that moment of her being his at his bidding—were more than she could take.

Raw emotion seared painfully through her and she jerked

away from him, hiding her stricken face from his view. 'Well, you certainly know how to cool a girl's ardour!' she managed in a fairly credible voice—and positively flew out of there. Her self-control was in tatters, but even so, it was unthinkable that she should break down in front of him.

# CHAPTER SEVEN

It was only later, much later, when she was back in her home again, that Romillie wondered if she could have handled matters better. Had she not been in that highly emotionally charged state to begin with, would she have been better able to cope differently with what she had, in that state, seen as Naylor's rejection of her?

But she *had* been up there in that summit of non-thinking, feeling only raw emotion—and what had happened *had* happened. And even now she could not honestly say whether she was glad or sorry that, though they had come close, she and Naylor had not actually made love.

Which made her wonder where on earth was her pride?

Thankfully, she had managed to find sufficient of it to eventually come out from the bathroom with her head held high. Naylor had not been impressed. Why would he have been? He had been holding a responsive, more than willing female in his arms—a female who had been giving him go, go, go signs all the way. Then, his emotions stretched too, wham, she had rocketed away, leaving him wanting.

It was no wonder that he had been monstrously aloof to her the next time he saw her. Without a word being said—forget the way she liked her eggs—he had taken her to the hospital, checked on the situation with regard to Lewis, paid him a quick visit, had a courteous word with her mother and, doing away with the pretence of an affectionate parting to Romillie for her mother's benefit, not so much as a peck on the cheek had he given her. He had gone on his way.

Fortunately Eleanor Fairfax had had other matters on her mind, not least her fiancé's health, and had not noticed.

Lewis, it had been confirmed, had suffered a mild heart attack. But he was doing well, and it was unlikely he would be hospitalised for too long.

'I don't want him to be on his own when he's free to leave here,' Eleanor stated. 'I'd like him to come and stay with us, Rom, if you don't mind.'

'Of course I don't mind,' Romillie answered.

'I think he needs a bit of spoiling, and if he goes back to his place, there will be no one there to look after him.'

'You don't have to explain,' Romillie replied, giving her a hug. If anything of the same sort happened to Naylor, God forbid, she would not want anyone else to look after him but herself.

Not that he would ever call on her to do anything for him. He was his own man, was Naylor Cardell, and wanted help from no one—'I really will have to consider marrying you' he had mocked. Oh, how those words still wounded.

She wanted to see him again, but did not want to see him again. It was the 'did not' side of her that determined to keep out of his way; not that he showed any signs of having a breakdown over it. It was for sure he had not tried to make contact with her. And, remembering the cold and aloof way he had been with her, she knew that he never would.

It was because she was afraid she might bump into him at the hospital that Romillie kept well away. She dropped her mother off at the railway station on Saturday and Sunday and was there to meet her when she came home again in the early evening.

She was delighted to see that her mother's new-found confidence was showing no sign of diminishing. It had grown so much, in fact, that on the Friday, Saturday and Sunday, when she returned from visiting Lewis, Romillie had sat beside her in the car while Eleanor brushed up on her dormant driving skills. The idea being that, with Lewis being advised to not drive for a while, she would be able to drive him out and about and thereby, as she put it, prevent him from going 'stir crazy'.

Her mother had news to tell her when Romillie picked her up from the station on Monday. Romillie barely had the chance to ask after Lewis's progress before she was joyously beaming, 'Lewis is coming home tomorrow!'

'He's well enough?'

'Isn't it incredible? Less than a week ago I was in panic that... Well, it really doesn't bear thinking about. And now, tomorrow...'

'It is wonderful,' Romillie said sincerely. And offered, 'Would you like me to get some time off to go and collect him?'

'That's sweet of you, darling. But Naylor popped in while I was there and he volunteered to drive him here.'

Ooh—difficult! For herself, Romillie knew she would make herself scarce and so avoid having to see him. Against that, though, she did not want Lewis to think that he was not welcome; so from that point of view, and the manners of the thing, she would have to come straight home from work and not find an excuse to keep out of the way.

'There's no need for Naylor to do that,' she replied. 'With Lewis out of action Naylor must be endlessly busy with his work, without taking precious time out of his day to drive down here.'

'That's what I said, but Naylor wouldn't hear of it. The other good news is that, having had time to think about it, and I think this little heart attack scare helped him to make up his mind, Lewis has decided to retire as of now.'

'He's giving up the chairmanship?'

'Lewis says that Naylor is more than competent to take over, and he has the full backing of the board.'

'And—Naylor has agreed?'

'He'll probably tell you all this himself, but Lewis says, given that Naylor will be doing two jobs—his and Lewis's—before he can delegate some of the lesser responsibility—and he had been doing more and more before Lewis was taken ill,' Eleanor inserted, going on, 'and with Naylor being so busy he hasn't been able to see you at all over the weekend, it's only natural that he'll snatch a moment to come over as soon as he can. Driving Lewis here is—'

'Mother!' Romillie was horrified at the way her parent's thoughts were going.

'I know, I know, it's too soon yet, but it's obvious to me that he cares for you.'

Romillie realised then that, since that was the impression she and Naylor, in the interests of getting her mother and Lewis to spend time together in different places—had been trying to give, she could hardly blame her for thinking what she did. But now, while she was so delighted at the thought of Lewis coming home to her, did not seem the moment to confess what a sham it all was.

Lewis's room was all ready for him, and her mother was starting to look a little uptight when Romillie went home at lunchtime the following day. She had been half hoping that Naylor would have been and gone by the time she got there—even while part of her cried out to see him.

'Should I put flowers in his room, do you think?' Eleanor asked. 'I don't want Lewis to think I'm fussing.'

'Do you want to put flowers in his room?'

'Yes, I do.'

'Then do it, love,' Romillie urged. 'Lewis loves you because you're you, and because of the way you think and feel.'

All of a sudden Eleanor relaxed, and laughed self-consciously. 'For a while there I was back to being sixteen.'

Naylor's car was parked on the drive when Romillie arrived home shortly after five. Just to see his car and to know he was there caused warm emotional colour to burn her skin, making her glad she knew he was in the house before she went in. With luck her colour would be normal by the time she saw him again.

She tried a little deep breathing—it did not help. Her insides were all of a mish-mash when, knowing if they had heard the car she could delay no longer, she opened the door and went along to the sitting room.

She flicked a glance to somewhere near Naylor's chin, her lips smiling as she went straight to Lewis and kissed his cheek before standing back and looking at him. To her mind he looked exactly the same as he always had.

'I'm glad you're staying with us,' she greeted him.

His eyes went to her mother. 'So am I,' he said.

Because it was expected of her to say something to Naylor, she turned to him, 'Congratulations on your appointment,' she managed calmly. Oh, how dear he was to her.

'It isn't official yet,' he replied evenly.

'It soon will be,' Lewis put in, and as Romillie turned away, and conversation centred briefly on Lewis retiring and Naylor taking over, for all her heart was banging clamorously away she was through her initial moments of panic.

She looked at him as he conversed easily with her mother. She looked at his wonderful face in profile. He half turned and she looked at his sensational mouth. It seemed utterly incredible, unreal somehow, that less than a week ago she had lain in his bed, he had kissed her and aroused in her undreamed-of emotions.

He turned his head a fraction, flicking a glance to her and instantly away again. Then, as if he too could hardly believe that she had been in his bed, warm and wanting, he flicked another glance at her, that glance moving briefly to her mouth.

Then suddenly, as if he had just remembered he had matters to attend to, he was saying he must get back. And Romillie did not want him to go, not yet. She felt starved for the sight of him.

But pride reared up. Quite obviously Naylor could not wait

to be gone. 'You won't stay and have a meal with us?' she enquired, not knowing what she would do if he said yes.

'Things to do,' he apologised.

And was rewarded with her best phoney smile. 'Of course,' she said, and knew from that almost imperceptible glint that came to his steady blue eyes that he had seen her phoney smile for what it was, and was impressed neither by it nor her.

She did not see Naylor again after that. She had not expected that she would. It was from Lewis, who apparently phoned him daily, that she learned anything that there was to learn; though as the days passed that was not very much. The news that his chairmanship was official was commented on in the press. Other news filtered through. Naylor had moved offices. He was taking his PA with him. Naylor was busy, busy, busy. It was on the cards that Naylor would have to go abroad for a while.

'Are you and Naylor all right?' he mother asked one day. 'I don't mean to pry, but…'

She looked concerned, but Romillie did not want the smallest thing to put a blight on her happiness, and just could not find the words to tell her that she and Naylor were— nothing. 'We're fine,' she answered cheerfully. Time enough to tell her the truth about her and Naylor. Well, some of the truth anyway. There were parts of her knowing Naylor, of their being together, that were intensely private. 'You know how busy he is,' she excused.

'He won't always be busy,' Eleanor consoled. 'Just while the changeover is happening.'

'I can't believe how well Lewis looks.' Romillie changed the subject. Her mother was instantly side-tracked.

'He's making a marvellous recovery,' she sighed. And confessed, 'I truly had not appreciated just how much he meant to me until that phone call from Naylor from the hospital and I feared I might lose him.'

'So when's the wedding?'

Eleanor laughed sunnily. Lewis had popped next door to take one last look around his cousin's house before he handed the whole business over to the estate agent. 'Soon,' she answered, but was serious all at once as she confided, 'Lewis wants me to go and take a look at his home tomorrow, so that we can decide if we want to live here, there, or purchase a property elsewhere.' And, while that her mother might want to leave the only home she had ever known had somehow not occurred to Romillie, Eleanor was going on, 'You'll come with us tomorrow, of course. Naturally we want you to have a say in where we all live.'

'Oh, Mum, I don't think so,' Romillie replied. She instinctively knew that, kind though both Lewis and her mother were being, and apart from the fact she thought they should start off their married life together just the two of them, the time had come to do some thinking about her own future.

'It's Saturday, there's nothing to prevent you from coming with us,' Eleanor protested.

'You want me to drive?'

'No, no, it's not that. But I want you involved, darling. And Lewis agrees with me.' She looked a little moist-eyed as she continued, 'It's only now, now that I feel strong and me again, that I can see what a terrible load I must have put on your young shoulders.'

'Oh, come on, you weren't that bad,' Romillie teased. 'But I'd planned to do a wardrobe sort-out tomorrow.' And, when her mother still looked doubtful, 'I can go with you and have a look at Lewis's home after you've decided where you want to live.'

Romillie did not feel very much like wardrobe-sorting the following morning, but, having waved her mother and Lewis off, thought it might make her less of a fibber if she followed through with the idea.

She was upstairs in her bedroom, deep in thought about how astonishingly confident her mother now was, and accepting that her role as her mother's protector was now redundant.

Time to let go, Romillie realised. Lewis would soon be as good as new, and she knew that as her mother would take good care of him, so Lewis would take good care of her mother.

Romillie, beyond endorsing that she did not think it right that she live with them, had not got as far as deciding what she could do about her future when she heard a car on the drive.

Her heart leapt, and she took a quick look out of the window. It was her father's car. Disappointment hit her like a physical blow. Though why she had thought her visitor might be Naylor just showed her what a hold he had on her.

She went downstairs—her father had let himself in, and she was glad that her mother and Lewis were not home. What Lewis did not need to see in this stage of his recovery was her father in one of his rages—even though it was doubtful that her father would have tried bullying her mother with another male present.

'Mum's not in,' she greeted him when they met in the hall.

'I'll come in and wait,' he said, pushing past her and, as if he owned the place, going to take his ease on the sitting room sofa.

'Would you like coffee?' Romillie offered—he was, after all, her father. At least she could be civil to him.

'How long's your mother going to be?' he demanded.

Romillie's protective instincts came out in full force. Perhaps it would be as well if her mother moved away. That way, at least, she would be spared the upsetting spasmodic visits from her former husband.

'Hours, I should think.'

Archer Fairfax looked surprised. 'Where's she gone? She never goes out!' he exclaimed, and clearly wanted to know more.

Had she thought for a moment that he had any lingering caring for her mother, Romillie might have dressed it up a little. But the only person Archer Fairfax cared about was Archer Fairfax, so Romillie told him straight, 'My mother is getting married again.'

'She's—what?' He looked staggered. 'Who's she marrying?' he demanded.

'A very nice man,' Romillie replied, but saw the irony of her remark was lost on him as, staggered or no by the news, it did not take him long to think only of number one.

'Where are they going to live?' he questioned, his eyes already going possessively around the sitting room.

'Um…' Romillie hesitated. 'They're not sure.'

'Your mother might move to his place?' he questioned slyly.

'It's—er—possible.'

'Then I'd better move back in here,' he decided without further ado. 'It'll be much too lonely for you here on your own.'

His concern was touching! He had never bothered that she might be lonely before. His visit made her feel uncomfortable in her own home, and Romillie was not sorry when eventually he must have realised that there was nothing to be gained at the moment by staying, and decided to go.

She was back upstairs, tidying up in her bedroom and wondering how much she should tell her mother, while realising she could not keep her father's visit a secret, when the phone rang.

Naylor, she thought, but that was because he was usually her first thought anyway. She tripped lightly down the stairs to answer it—ready to say she was not the George Hotel—and discovered that it *was* Naylor.

She had to swallow hard before she could speak, but her voice still came out all choked-up nevertheless. 'Lewis isn't here at the moment,' she told Naylor, it being a foregone conclusion that he had not rung to speak to her. 'He and my mother have gone over to Lewis's home.'

'You sound a bit—upset?' Naylor commented stiffly—obviously still not having forgiven her for so abruptly changing the green light a screeching red stop light.

Oh, grief! 'My father has just visited.'

'You're all right?' Naylor demanded sharply. 'He didn't—'

'I'm fine!' she interrupted him. 'He's gone now, anyway.' And, needing an explanation for her choked-up voice, 'But his visits are always upsetting to some degree.' And, wanting to get away from the subject, 'How are you?' she enquired politely—in a voice that came into the same category as her phoney smile.

'About to go to the airport,' he replied coolly, clearly not thinking very much of her polite enquiry.

'Lewis mentioned you were going abroad.'

'Just for a couple of weeks,' he commented, the politeness bug having bitten him too she realised, and after the way they had been together, she was not thanking him for it either.

'Have a good trip,' she bade him.

End of conversation. She was left holding the phone in her hand. But at least his call had taken her father's visit from her mind for a while.

Though his visit was something she could not keep to herself when her mother and Lewis returned. But, because she did not want Lewis to be upset in any way, she waited until he had gone upstairs to stow the suitcase of some of his belongings and other impedimenta that he had taken the opportunity to collect while in his home.

'Have you decided?' Romillie asked.

'Lewis has a lovely home, without a draught or a leak, and there is space to have a studio built on. But we've decided to mull it over for a few days. Besides which, I want you to see it before we finally decide.'

Romillie did not think it was the right moment just then to tell her that, should they decide to move, she would not be moving with them. 'Dad called,' she blurted out instead.

Her mother looked across at her sharply. 'Was he all right?' she asked, sounding concerned.

'I told him you were getting married.'

'And?' Eleanor queried, experience of Archer Fairfax telling her that there was more to it than that.

'Basically,' Romillie began lightly, 'he thinks that if you're moving out, he should move in—so I won't be lonely on my own.'

Eleanor stood stock still. But, where once just the knowledge that he had been in the house would have been sufficient to make her crumple, this time she drew a deep breath and literally squared up her shoulders. 'I,' she said succinctly, 'have had just about enough of him.' And while Romillie stood rooted, amazed again at the way all sign of the timid creature she had been had been washed away from her mother since she had known Lewis, she went straight over to the phone and picked it up. 'What's your father's number?' she asked.

'It's in the index,' Romillie answered, mesmerized, before going into action and finding the number for her.

Without more ado, as Romillie watched in stunned silence, her mother stabbed out the digits. 'Eleanor!' she announced bluntly when the phone was answered. 'I'm ringing to inform you of several matters.' And charging on, not heeding anything he might have to say, 'One. I do not want you or your car on my driveway ever again. Should you decide to ignore that request, then I shall not hesitate to have you and it removed. Two. I am selling this house, so you can forget any idea of moving back in here before you start. Three. Any and *all* monies gained in the selling of my property will be immediately put into a trust fund for Romillie—where I will be the chief trustee. Which will mean that *you* will never see a penny of it.' There followed a pause in which Romillie, from where she stood, could hear her father protesting on all decibels. Then her mother, like a lioness protecting her cub, was butting in again. 'You leave Romillie alone! Anything else you want to say to me can be said through our lawyers!' With that, she ended the call.

Wow! Shades of Grandfather Mannion in full throttle!! Feeling staggered, Romillie stared speechlessly at her mother. It was taking some getting used to, this transformation in her from the person she had been as little as three months ago.

'What?' Eleanor asked, on catching her gaping at her.

Romillie quickly gathered herself together. 'Um—you're not, are you?' she exclaimed after some moments.

'Not what?'

'Selling the house?' Romillie answered, not sure which had shaken her more—this new-found assertive mother, or the fact she had spoken of putting the house up for sale.

'Darling, of course not,' Eleanor laughed. 'The house is yours, you know that, regardless of what we decide to do.' She laughed again. 'But suddenly, out of nowhere, I felt a little bit empowered—it's taken a long while to get here, I must admit. But all at once I saw no reason, after all the lies Archie Fairfax has told me in his day, why I should not tell him a few of my own.'

Romillie stared at her in wonderment. 'But—you never tell lies!' she exclaimed incredulously. Indeed, if asked, she would have sworn that her mother was incapable of telling a lie.

'That's true, I don't,' Eleanor agreed. But then some thought must have come to her, because all at once Romillie could see that she was looking more than a touch ill at ease. 'Er…' She stumbled, but obviously felt that she had to go on. 'I—um—may not have been able to tell you an outright lie, but—er—I have to confess to one occasion when I was extremely—er—evasive.'

Romillie continued to stare at her. Something was not right here! In particular with her mother's use of the term 'may not have been able to tell you an outright lie.' It sounded very much as if she had come pretty close to lying to her on one occasion.

Even so, Romillie was convinced that it could not have been as bad as all that. 'When was this?' she asked lightly. And, starting to smile, 'What have you done?' she enquired.

'It's more what I haven't done. More what I should have said, but didn't,' Eleanor replied, and was back to being defensive again, which Romillie never again wanted to see. 'I didn't want you to be embarrassed in any kind of way—and we did desperately need the money.'

Romillie tried to keep up. Tried to think when last they had desperately needed some money. It did not need too much thinking about. Her father had been involved then; he had taken all their money and she had been ready to sell the car. Only she hadn't had to sell the car because…

'That would be around the time you sold a couple of your paintings,' she began. 'The one that used to hang in the hall and—'

'They weren't both paintings,' her mother cut in quietly. 'I let you think they were because—'

'Because you didn't want me to be—embarrassed, you said, in any kind of way?' Romillie butted in quietly, before, her brain going into overdrive, shock, sudden and abrupt, hit her four-square. If only one of the sales had been a painting… 'One was a—sketch?' she guessed faintly, as everything that had so far been said began to take shape. 'A new—a recent sketch?'

'One was a sketch,' Eleanor admitted. 'The sketch of you— the nude,' she went on hurriedly. 'But you mustn't worry about it, darling. He told me he had absolutely no intention of putting it on display, and…'

'Who…?' Romillie began, her voice slightly cracked. 'Who bought it?' Rampant suspicion charged through her. Her mother had, misleadingly, said that someone she had met at the art exhibition they had attended had bought it. But Romillie, trying not to panic, was getting the most horrendous vibes that she knew the identity of the purchaser. No! She couldn't bear it if…

'Well, naturally I wouldn't have sold it to just anybody. And I'm sure he would eventually have told you himself—only he's been so busy, so tied up with business matters. Anyhow, Naylor said…'

What else her mother said after that barely penetrated. All Romillie could think of was how Naylor had told her, the second time she had met him, that he did not want to buy that sketch—his exact words when she had told him that the sketch was not for sale, had been, 'Strangely enough, I wasn't thinking of buying it'.

'Are you very upset, Rom?' Eleanor asked tentatively.

And from somewhere Romillie found a smile. And somehow too, when she would have thought 'absolutely mortified' better described how she was feeling, rather than plain 'upset', she managed to rise above her inner feelings. She never wanted her mother on the defensive ever again.

'Shaken, perhaps,' she agreed, and, able when the occasion demanded to lie too, she found a mammoth one to assure her, 'But if we had to sell it, I'd rather Naylor bought it than anyone. He rang while you were out, by the way.'

Eleanor instantly looked relieved that she was taking it so well that she had gone on to talk about something else. 'Of course he did,' she said softly. 'It must be very irksome to him that he is so up to his eyes in it that he won't have time to come and see you before he goes away. But fourteen days will soon pass,' she went on, sounding more at ease. 'And then he'll be back again. He rang Lewis while we were at his home, and after the call Lewis was saying how everything will settle down soon and Naylor will have more free time.'

As soon as she could, without giving away that she seriously needed to be by herself, Romillie escaped to her room. Naylor would be away for two weeks, but she knew that, were he to be away for two whole months, two years, even, she still would not be ready to see him again.

She hardly knew which was the bigger embarrassment: the fact that he had that nude sketch of her and could take it out and look at it any time he chose, or the fact that he had only bought it because he had known they were broke—she had told him herself that she was thinking of selling the car.

She sighed heavily, realising that since he had not wanted the sketch in the first place he was more likely to have tossed it in a drawer and forgotten all about it, so she had little to be embarrassed about there. But what was more cringingly embarrassing was the fact that, knowing they were on their uppers, he had sought and found a way to help them financially. She had made him promise not to tell Lewis any of what had gone on. This, she saw, had been Naylor's way of helping them in Lewis's stead.

And it was embarrassing, more than embarrassing. She did not know if her pride would ever recover.

It did not get any better. Sunday came, and she was still being assaulted by the thought that on the Monday following their leaving his Cotswolds home the day before Naylor, having observed Lewis's feeling for her mother, had called at their home with the express intention of finding some way—from his respect and friendship with Lewis—of making their lives easier, of making them solvent again and free from money worries.

All through the week that followed Romillie could not get out of her head the humiliating knowledge of what Naylor had done, and why he had done it. On one level she supposed she should be grateful to him that his intervention had saved them from having to part with the car. But they would have managed somehow. They would have had to have done.

She got up on Saturday morning and felt so restless she found it impossible to settle. She padded around her bedroom, feeling like a lost soul. Perhaps it wouldn't feel so bad if she did not love Naylor so much.

Briefly she wondered if he had maybe been thinking of her just a little when he had made his art purchases. He had been aware that her worries had set her off on the sleepwalking track again. Had he decided to eliminate her worries...?

Oh, for goodness' sake! Impatient with herself for being so needy, for looking for the smallest sign that Naylor had a crumb of caring for her, Romillie left her room. A spirit of restlessness went with her.

That feeling persisted all morning, but it was after lunch when such an uproar of overwhelming restless loneliness attacked that when her mother queried, 'Are you all right, darling? You're looking awfully pale!' Romillie knew she needed to be doing something, anything.

'Nothing that a little fresh air won't cure,' she answered brightly.

'Cooped up behind that reception desk all week doesn't help,' Eleanor agreed. 'Lewis and I are going for a long steady walk later. Why don't you come with us?'

'I was thinking more of taking a drive somewhere,' Romillie answered on the spur of the moment, feeling more that she would want to gallop from this love that was eating at her than take a steady walk. 'Will you need the car if I don't get back for a few hours?'

It was around two o'clock when Romillie set off. At that point she had no particular aim in mind other than to motor around and hope that, with her mind concentrated on her driving, perhaps she would not have space to dwell on Naylor, her love for him, the loneliness of that love, and the giant swathe of embarrassment that followed her around, threatening to suffocate her.

It had been a faint hope, a ridiculous hope, she realised some while later—Naylor was with her every mile of the way.

She had no idea how many miles she had motored, or where in creation she was. But then suddenly, having taken random see-where-this-gets-you twists and turns, she found she had turned off a main road and onto a minor road—a road that was slightly familiar.

She gave a half-groan as she recognised suddenly that this road led towards Naylor's home, Oaklands! For a moment she went hot all over, and very nearly executed a rapid about-turn. Then it was that she remembered that Naylor was out of the country, and she motored on for several miles more, no longer wondering at this inbuilt radar she seemed to have that had brought her so close to the place where she had spent a happy time with him.

If she was not mistaken, just up ahead was that lane she had walked down with Naylor that Saturday. She slowed the car, wanting to drive on by, but finding that she could not. There was a special place at the end of that lane—a place where she and Naylor had lingered in complete harmony.

She was still driving slowly when she spotted a clearing just opposite the top of the lane. It seemed to be a place where winter road grit was heaped. It was now empty. Before she knew it Romillie had pulled over onto it. She parked her car and got out, knowing only then that she wanted to relive again those minutes where she had strolled down that lane with Naylor.

It was such a peaceful day, and she walked slowly down the lane, halting now and again to study the foliage of the hedges, everywhere quiet except for the occasional birdsong. She was in no hurry. Naylor was miles and miles away.

She came to the end of the lane and saw again the lovely view of hills, trees of every sort, and there in particular, down at the stream's edge, those overhanging willows.

She didn't have to think about it, but as if compelled, simply made her way down, skirting round the one large willow to stand under it, gazing at the stream. For an age she stood there, studying the peacefulness of the scene and trying to find peace within herself.

But it was no good. Perhaps in time everything within her inner self would settle, even though that restlessness had shown not the smallest sign of leaving her.

Yet she wanted to stay, did not want to go. But, since common sense decreed she could not stay there for ever, Romillie reluctantly decided she had better go back to her car.

Before she could move from her half-hidden spot beneath the willow tree, however, she heard a sound that alerted her to the fact that she might not be alone.

Hurriedly she spun about—just as a masculine hand parted the hanging foliage. Scalding hot colour scorched her face—breath left her in a gasp of shock, of amazement—and not a little panic.

Striking blue eyes looked directly into hers. 'I thought it was your car back there,' Naylor said easily, those steady blue eyes taking in her fiery blush. 'Tell me, Romillie,' he began mildly, 'what are you doing here?'

She was in shock still, and racked her brain that had suddenly gone brainless for any answer. He should be in Portugal or somewhere. Certainly not here!

'I want that sketch!' she exclaimed forcefully, the embarrassment in her soul taking over from her witless head.

If Naylor was surprised by her blunt statement, he hid it well. He rocked back slightly on his heels—though did not pretend to not know what she was talking about. 'You can't afford it,' he replied evenly.

That did not help her feelings of embarrassment in the smallest. 'I come into some money when I'm twenty-five. I'll double what you paid for it,' she said recklessly.

Naylor studied her for long seconds, and she would have given anything to know what he was thinking. But at long last he stretched out a hand and fully parted the willow, to give her space to walk through.

'This place is too nice a place in which to talk business,' he commented. 'Come up to the house,' he invited, 'we'll discuss it there.'

No way, said her head. What's to discuss? She walked through the opening he had made, and he moved to one side. Yes, said her heart.

# CHAPTER EIGHT

BY THE time they had reached the top of the lane her head was firmly in control once more. No way was she going to go up to his house with him.

Romillie took her car keys out from her pocket and went to walk over to her car. 'We'll go in my car.' Naylor forestalled her intent, taking a firm hold of her arm and guiding her over to his vehicle—every bit as if he knew what was in her mind.

Though why he would bother if she just got in her car and simply drove off, she couldn't think. But the feel of his hand on her arm was weakening, and anyway she told herself it would be undignified to struggle.

'It's a nice day for a walk!' she commented loftily, meaning she would not need him to give her a lift back down to her car after their 'discussion'.

Nerves started to get to her, however, once she was seated in his car next to him. Just being with him was blowing her mind. She tried hard to concentrate on matters sensible.

'You finished your business early?' she enquired politely. But Naylor was already shaking his head.

'I had a meeting this morning, but decided to come home for a few hours. I have to go back tomorrow.'

His world, she realised, was vastly different from hers. If in the unlikely event of a dental receptionist needing to go abroad on business, it was a certainty she would stay there until that business was completed.

'You've just come from the airport?' she guessed, observing the lightweight business suit he wore. And, before he could answer, 'Drop me off here, Naylor,' she requested. 'You've been talking business all week. You must want a rest now you're home.'

He carried on driving, zapped open the electronic gates to his home and steered his vehicle up the long drive. That was when it hit her full force that the only reason a man of his virile energy would take a break and fly home must be because he had serious other plans for his free time.

'You've a heavy date tonight, haven't you?' she blurted out in a very sharp accusatory rush—and was instantly appalled.

Naylor halted the car—she absently noted that they had arrived at his front door. But he made no move to leave the car, turning to her, his look thoughtful. 'Do you know, Romillie, for a moment there you sounded quite jealous?' he commented, his eyes searching her face.

'Pfff!' she scorned explosively. 'If you believe that, you'll believe anything.' And with that, feeling hot all over, she turned the door handle and stepped out of the car.

Because there was little else she could do, although if she were honest there was little else she wanted to do, Romillie went with him into his house.

'Would you like coffee?' he asked as they entered the drawing room.

'Not particularly,' she replied, in view of her near disaster in the jealousy department a short while ago, determined to keep this as non-personal as she could. Though that was ruined in an instant when the weakening thought struck of how he must have been travelling for hours and, when he wanted nothing more than to relax, unwind, she was invading his home. 'But I'll make you some if you want to put your feet up for five minutes.'

Naylor smiled a smile that all but melted her backbone. 'I

wouldn't mind getting out of my work clothes,' he said of his immaculate suit.

To her way of thinking what they had to discuss would not take more than five minutes, certainly not long enough to warrant her waiting around while he got out of his suit. But if he wanted to change, who was she to argue?

She left him and, feeling more than a little amazed to find herself in Naylor's kitchen making coffee, knew that she must not stay any longer than it took to perhaps drink a cup of coffee and to hopefully negotiate the return of that sketch.

Romillie was in the middle of congratulating herself that she had scornfully succeeded in covering what she had to admit had been a moment of raw and absolute jealousy earlier when, casual trouser-clad, casual shirt—and handsome with it—Naylor strolled into the kitchen.

'That smells good,' he remarked of the aroma of coffee percolating.

'It won't be long,' Romillie replied, and felt all sort of jittery all of a sudden. What she did not need was that Naylor should not only notice it, but refer to it.

'What's wrong?' he asked, leaning against one of the units and looking directly at her.

'Wrong?' she queried evasively, flicking him a sideways look.

'You seem—nervous?'

'Me?' She tried to bluff—then gave it up. 'It's you!' She threw the ball back into his court.

'Me?' he queried. 'What did I do?'

Short of telling him that what he had done had been to make her fall in love with him, and that part of what was wrong was the history they had between them—had he so soon forgotten that fairly unleashed passion they had shared in his bed?—she could find no answer.

'I thought we were friends, Romillie,' he pursued, when she had not spoken.

'You've a funny way of showing friendship!' she flared, in spite of her determination to stay cool and calm.

'You mean our making love that—'

'No, I don't mean that!' she interrupted hurriedly, colour rushing to her face. Trust him to bring that up!

'What, then?'

'Coffee's ready.'

'What, then?' he insisted.

'You! You blow hot and cold,' she accused, perhaps a little unfairly, since she had done a little of blowing hot and cold herself, but she was suddenly feeling backed into a corner.

He considered her for a few long, unnerving moments, then, with a hint of humour in his eyes, 'I'll take half the blame if you'll take the other half,' he allowed.

Romillie wasn't sure where this conversation was going, or even if she wanted this conversation. 'Do you want coffee or not?' she demanded grumpily.

'Are you taking sugar in yours today?' he enquired nicely, and she hated him that, at his suggestion that she needed something to sweeten her up, she had to smile.

'That's better,' he said softly, bone-meltingly softly.

She did not trust herself to speak, but set about pouring a couple of cups of coffee. Naylor had other things on his mind too, she observed, as he took their coffee through to the drawing room.

He said not another word, anyhow, until they were both seated on sofas with a table at an angle in between. Then, pausing to take a swallow of his coffee, he looked across to her, a direct kind of glint in his blue eyes. 'I must say it's a pleasure to see you here, Rom,' he commented.

Her heart turned over, a burst of sheer joy erupting inside her at his words. Instantly, however, she had to remind herself that his words meant nothing except that perhaps, having witnessed her nervousness, he was attempting to put her at her ease.

'You know why I'm here,' she replied, marvelling that her voice sounded so even.

He looked at her levelly, then quite deliberately commented, 'I was hoping you had driven here because you couldn't keep away.'

Her mouth fell open in shock. She closed it and concentrated on her coffee cup while she got herself together. He was so close to the truth. She hadn't been able to keep away. Even if she had not acknowledged it, that subconscious part of her had known it.

'Honestly!' she derided. Then got stuck on his word 'hoping'. She shot a quick glance to him. Naylor had said he was *hoping* she was there because she couldn't keep away! Surely not? She pulled herself together. 'You know I'm here about that sketch and for no other reason,' she informed him firmly, attempting to put him straight.

Only, instead of doing anything of the kind, her words only succeeded in bringing a hint of a smile to his wonderful mouth. 'Dear, dear, Romillie,' he murmured softly, 'you didn't even know I was on my way home. You thought I was out of the country and would be away for another week.'

'I…' she tried to bluster, but her mind was a blank.

'I didn't even know myself that I'd be home today,' Naylor stated.

'Yes, well…' Oh, confound it, where was her brain when she needed it? 'You only decided to come home on the spur of the moment?' She attempted to sidetrack him.

'I couldn't stay away any longer,' he replied quietly.

'Well—um—Oaklands is rather lovely,' she commented, and went wittering on, 'It must pull you back time and time again.'

'It wasn't my home that was the appeal this time,' he answered.

And Romillie was sure she was not the smallest bit interested in which of his female companions was the lure. Though, bearing in mind how instantly Naylor had picked up that note of jealousy in her voice, she knew she had to be extra careful.

'About that sketch.' She abruptly took the conversation where she wanted to take it.

'Eleanor told you she'd let me have it?'

'My mother doesn't know yet that there is nothing between you and me—'

'Isn't there?' he cut in.

She wished he wouldn't. She knew full well he was refer-ring to the kisses they had shared that had gone beyond the bounds of simple friendship. 'I haven't been able to find an ap-propriate moment yet to confess how you and I have pretended to—er—be—um—getting on famously,' she said hurriedly. 'So my mother—' She broke off. 'Lewis can't know either, or he would have told my mother by now, surely?'

'I haven't told Lewis that my feelings for you are not anything but genuine.' Naylor settled that query.

'So, anyhow,' Romillie ploughed on, 'when...' She quite simply forgot what she had been saying. It was all his fault. 'Where was I?' she had to ask.

'Eleanor decided to tell you I was the purchaser...'

Oh, yes. 'She didn't actually decide,' Romillie took up. 'My father called while my mother and Lewis were over at Lewis's home.'

'You were upset after your father's visit,' Naylor recalled.

'Er...' Now did not seem the time to confess that it had been more hearing Naylor's voice so unexpectedly that had caused her to use her father as an excuse. 'Anyhow, I felt I had to tell my mother that he'd called, and also how I'd told him that she was getting married. My mother knows him well enough to know he'd look for some way to make capital out of that.'

'He found it?'

Somehow it did not seem disloyal to be talking to Naylor this way about her father. Though it was sadly true that her father had never done anything to deserve undying loyalty. 'He thought, if my mother was going to live elsewhere, that he should move back to save me from being lonely.'

'Is he going to move back in?' Naylor questioned sharply.

'No way!' Suddenly Romillie was smiling. 'Hardly had the words left my mouth than my mother was on the phone giving him what for. It was astonishing, Naylor,' she confided, still feeling slightly amazed. 'I've seen such a change in her since she has known Lewis, but that day she was truly magnificent, with no sign of a timid mouse about her as she told my father in no uncertain terms that she was selling the house and that the proceeds were straight away going into a trust fund for me—which she would make sure he never saw a penny of.'

'Is she—selling the house?'

'That's what I asked,' Romillie answered. 'I was still gaping at this new woman my mother had become when she laughed and told me that, with my father having told her so many lies, she didn't see why she shouldn't tell him a few for a change. The thing is,' Romillie went on, 'my mother never tells lies. If asked, I'd have said she just doesn't know how to tell a lie. I mentioned this to her, and that was when she confessed that, if she had not told me an outright lie, she had been extremely evasive when she'd allowed me to believe she had sold two of her paintings.'

'She confessed one of them was a sketch?'

Romillie nodded. 'At first I think I was able to cover my dismay—I just couldn't bear for her to be upset now that she's so happy—but I don't know which embarrassed me more: the fact that you have that nude drawing or the fact that, purely because I'd told you we were more or less broke, you, from your regard for Lewis, had been to my home and bailed us out by purchasing at least one item I knew you had not the smallest interest in.'

Naylor put down his cup and saucer and leaned forward to

study her. 'What a delightfully mixed-up creature you truly are,' he said quietly.

'Mixed-up! How?' She had always thought of herself as being fairly logical.

'Well, for a start, I bought that drawing essentially because I wanted it.'

Romillie stared at him, very much taken aback. 'But you didn't want it. You said that night, when I told you that it wasn't for sale, that you weren't thinking of buying it. You—'

Something in Naylor's expression caused her to break off. Oddly, it seemed to her as if he had just made a decision about something. As if this was decision time.

She was still looking at him a trifle puzzled when, to make her blink in surprise, 'I lied,' he told her, point-blank. And, while she continued to stare at him, 'I'm afraid, little Romillie Fairfax, that there have been many occasions when I haven't been exactly honest with you.'

She did not like being lied to. Did not like being deceived—which made it a wonder to her that she was still sitting there and was not halfway down the drive by now. Yet she had not moved. If asked, she would have said that Naylor Cardell was one of the most truthful men on the planet. Indeed, to be holding down the job he was holding down gave witness to the fact that he must be a man of the highest integrity.

'You've—deceived me?' she stayed there to ask.

'I didn't want to,' he admitted. 'You'd made it plain you had little trust in men, that you thought most of them were deceivers. But as I saw it then—and I still can't see that I could have acted any other way in my intent to gain what I wanted—deception was the only way.'

Romillie was staring at him, mystified. She did not like the sound of this one little bit. 'What on earth did you want that would entail deceiving me?' she asked sharply.

And very nearly collapsed at his reply when, looking levelly at her, appearing to be the one a shade nervous now, Naylor took a long pull of breath and clearly said, 'You, Romillie Fairfax. I wanted you.'

She half rose from her seat, but sank back down again. Her lips formed a startled 'O'. 'You wanted…' she began faintly, but was then unsure that she wanted to pursue that question. She had, she rather thought, shown herself eager to be his on one never-to-be-forgotten occasion. 'I'm not sure I want to be friends with someone who tells me lies,' she managed shakily. 'Are we friends?' she asked, unsure of just about everything just then.

'More than friends, I hope,' he answered unhesitatingly.

That made her feel a little pink about her cheeks, but it was a tribute to the depth of her love for him that she had not yet bolted, was still there waiting to hear any explanation he might wish to give. Though in her book very little excused lying for the pure devilment of it.

'Is it usual in your sphere to lie to your friends?' she enquired, a shade acidly it was true.

'Bear with me, sweetheart,' Naylor requested, that 'sweetheart' alone knocking her off course before he said another word. 'To go back to the very start, I walked into that art gallery that very first time we met—and was absolutely pole-axed.'

'Yes?' she questioned, purely because she had no clue to what had pole-axed him.

'There you were,' he went on, 'totally different from what I had been expecting. Th—'

'Expecting?' she exclaimed. 'You *expected* to see me there?' Puzzlement wasn't the word for it. 'I thought you just happened to be there. That—' Naylor shaking his head made her break off.

'Even Lewis wasn't sure that you and Eleanor would be there. But prior to that Lewis, to my surprise after his rancorous marriage and subsequent vitriolic divorce, had confided that he had met, been reacquainted with, a very gentle woman whom he was keen to take out.' Naylor had Romillie's full attention as he continued, 'Unfortunately this very gentle woman, having been through a similar traumatic marriage as himself, was still at the recovery stage and only ever went out with her daughter. He was quite prepared to take the two of them out if need be—'

'But my mother wouldn't hear of it,' Romillie slotted in.

Naylor smiled that bone melting smile and, while she was striving to not be affected by it, continued, 'Lewis wondered, subject to Eleanor being in agreement, how I felt about making up a four one evening. No way, was my first reaction—I'd got better things to do with my evenings than spend one of them entertaining some boring plain Jane from the sticks. Given that in my regard for Lewis I would almost certainly later have agreed to help if I possibly could, I initially only agreed to look in on the art gallery that night and—'

'And take a look at this boring plain Jane who—'

Naylor held up his hand. 'Guilty, bigoted, you name it. I'm thoroughly ashamed.' To Romillie's mind he did not look particularly ashamed. 'So I thought I could spare two minutes,' he conceded. 'Little did I know as I walked into that exhibition that my whole life was about to change.'

'Really?' Romillie stared at him, intrigued, not to say fascinated—too fascinated to get up and leave anyhow.

'I saw you the moment I walked in. You, dear Romillie, stopped me dead in my tracks.'

She swallowed. He had a tender sort of look about him somehow. He had called her 'dear Romillie'. Her mouth went dry. 'I—did?' she managed quietly.

Naylor nodded. 'There you stood, heart-stoppingly lovely— I was totally spellbound.'

'Spellbound?' she murmured, her eyes glued to him.

'I thought you the most exquisite creature I had ever seen,' he went on, and she was the one who was spellbound. 'I,

Romillie, at that very moment,' he clearly stated, 'fell heart and soul in love with you.'

She felt faint—she had not heard him correctly. She blushed crimson with emotion. 'You're—um—still lying?' was the best she could come up with.

He shook his head. 'The truth only from now on, Romillie, I promise.'

She made desperate attempts to get her head back together. 'Th-that's why you were so awful to me that night, was it? Because you'd fallen in love with me at first sight?'

'You're going to give me a hard time, I can tell,' he murmured. But agreed, 'I couldn't believe myself that I was talking to you the way I was. It was my pride coming to my aid. I just couldn't believe that you hadn't been struck by the same thunderbolt that had just flattened me. Yet there you were, looking straight through me. I wasn't having that! I knew then that I'd better do some pretty swift mental footwork.'

'That's why you had a go at me, accusing me of being selfish?'

'It was unforgivable of me—I didn't believe a word of it, of course,' he owned. 'But all the time I'm sorting you out I'm wondering how in creation I can get you to come out with me—it was as plain as day you weren't the least bit interested in me. And then—' a hint of a grin touched his mouth '—there *you* are, inviting me to make up a foursome.'

'You were reluctant!' she recalled accusingly.

'I was overjoyed—and trying to hide it,' he countered, adding gently, 'That was the first of my deceptions.'

Had he really said that he loved her? She tried to steady her fast-beating heart. Or had that been a deception too? She felt confused suddenly, and while she so badly wanted to believe him did not know what to believe any more. But hadn't he just said, 'The truth only from now on'?

'You—um...' Her voice had gone husky on her. Her teachers at school had all said she had a good brain, and she attempted to use it, though acknowledged that her thinking might be a little wrecked by the feelings of love and emotion she was battling against. 'I can't remember seeing any evidence that you were— um—keen in any way,' she challenged. 'You didn't ring me or...'

'My impression was that you didn't even like me.'

'Well, perhaps not, to start with,' she conceded.

He smiled. 'So you *did* start to like me at some point?'

'You're much too smart!' she retorted sniffily.

'I've been in an agony of suspense,' he replied.

'You're looking for the sympathy vote.'

He burst out laughing. 'Now who's being smart?' She did not answer and he went on, 'I've had to bide my time, Romillie. It hasn't been easy.'

'How?' she wanted to know.

'I've had to wait,' he replied. 'When what I've wanted to do was to ring you ten times a day, I've had to wait for you to get in touch with me.'

She blinked, and recalled, 'I said I would ring about that foursome dinner.'

'And I was in hell, having to wait for your call.'

'But—you didn't sound very thrilled to hear from me,' she reminded him—with no intention of letting him, so to speak, pull the wool over her eyes.

'I was inwardly rejoicing.'

She looked at him sceptically. 'You made no move to see me again after that.'

'I intended to leave it a week and then perhaps casually stop by your home on my way to some invented place on Saturday. Then I didn't need to, because on Friday you rang and all of a sudden there's light at the end of my very dark tunnel when you invite me to a retirement dinner.' He frowned slightly as he recalled, 'Only I soon found out that you were not asking me for me, but on account of Davidson.'

'You were furious with me.'

'I was enraged, quietly seething. You'd made me emotion-ally vulnerable and I didn't like that either,' he admitted. 'Not to mention I was as jealous as hell.'

Romillie stared at him wide-eyed. 'Honestly?' she gasped.

'Truthfully,' he replied.

'You kissed me, first in anger and then…' She felt dreamy all of a sudden.

'You preferred the second kiss?' he fished gently.

'You made me want you,' she said, quite without thinking.

'Darling,' Naylor murmured, and leaving his seat, as if just a few yards away was too much of a distance, he came over and sat with her on the sofa.

He was about to take her in his arms, but she stopped him. *'Don't!'* she said sharply. 'I need to try and think clearly.' She quickly realised she had just about admitted that he had such an earth-shattering effect on her that her usual powers of thinking, of reasoning, were totally shot, so saw no point then in holding back. 'I cannot abide deception,' she went on, as calmly as she was able, 'and you've said the truth only from now on.'

'That's what I want,' he agreed. 'So—you wanted me that night?'

'It was a new experience for me.'

'Sweet love. And it worried you?'

'Only in so much as I feared I might have inherited my father's loose traits.'

'But when you'd worked it out—and realised that by no reckoning were you in any way morally like him—you sent me white roses. And I,' he said softly, 'fell more deeply in love with you than ever.'

'Oh, Naylor, don't say that if you don't mean it,' she begged.

'Lovely girl,' he breathed, and would have taken her in his arms. But she stiffened, and he, accepting that the time was not yet right, pulled back. 'I wanted to phone you without delay, but had to force myself to wait until Friday to phone and thank you.'

She wanted to stretch over and kiss him. But there was more at stake here than the comfort of the moment. She had no idea what sort of relationship Naylor wanted. Perhaps no sort of relationship at all. But, with traces of deception lurking in the air, she knew that for her a relationship or even a friendship based on deception was no relationship at all.

'Is that it? The extent of your deception of me?' she asked quietly.

'I love you,' he said. Unsmiling, she looked back at him, her heart beating nineteen to the dozen. 'My poor bruised flower,' he murmured, 'it's not enough is it? Your father has given you one hell of a complex about trust, hasn't he?'

Naylor's tone was weakening her. But she was not going to have her mother's life. 'I must be able to trust,' she answered painfully.

'I'll teach you to trust, little darling,' Naylor said softly. 'I'll break down those barriers built in your years of caring for Eleanor. Trust me, my reason for deceiving you in any way has only ever been because I need you to love me in return. Because of that I've had to pretend that I wasn't interested in you personally. But I took you to my sister's party for no other reason than—'

'Sophie...'

'An old friend. Charlie Todd?' he countered.

'Charlie Todd?'

'He was after your phone number—and I was all green-eyed again,' he confessed, going on, 'I've known Sophie for years—no history there. In any event, other women ceased to exist for me from that moment I first laid eyes on you.'

'I thought you wanted a platonic—er—friendship only,' she murmured.

'It's what I wanted you to believe. I wanted to get close to you. Get you to know me a little.' He smiled gently. 'I thought I could cope with platonic—I just hadn't taken into account the many times I would want to take you into my arms and just hold you and keep on holding you.'

'You did?' she asked, knowing she was playing for time, needing to think clearly, but suddenly finding she was in more of a fog.

'The whole time. I tried to keep everything platonic between us when, as much for me as for Lewis and Eleanor, I invited you here that weekend.'

'We kissed,' she recalled.

'And I never wanted to stop,' he replied, his eyes tender on hers.

'Oh, Naylor,' she cried, her voice all sort of wobbly.

'Love me?' he asked.

She could not lie. 'You know that I do,' she admitted.

He let go a relieved breath, but did not touch her. 'I'd hoped. Once or twice I thought I'd caught a glimpse... But then you'd go all cold on me—and I wouldn't know where the hell I was any more.'

'I know the feeling,' she owned, and saw a gentle smile for her break on his wonderful mouth.

'I've been in torment over you, Romillie,' he confessed. 'You've been in my head both night and day.' And, to make her eyes go huge, 'That's why I came home today.'

'B-because of me?' she gasped, staring at him flabbergasted.

'I couldn't take another week of the ache inside of me,' he replied. 'I organised a flight, and as soon as my meeting was finished I was off.'

'You were going to give me a ring? Call at the house?'

'I've already been there,' he revealed, to again shake her. 'Frustratingly, there was no one in. I looked through the side window of your garage—the car had gone. Even more frustratingly, I didn't know your mobile phone number, and Lewis wasn't answering his.'

'He and my mother planned to go for a long walk. Lewis probably left his phone at home.'

'Which was of no comfort when I left Tarnleigh, down-heartedly fearing that the three of you had gone away some-where for the weekend.'

'So you came on down here?'

'So I did, knowing as I drove that, when I'd considered I'd bided my time long enough, and must have something settled before I flew back tomorrow, I was just going to have to wait yet another unbearably long drawn-out week before I saw you again.'

'But—then you saw my car.'

'I couldn't believe it! I even got out of my car and went over and touched it.'

'It was no mirage.'

'No figment of my fevered imagination.' He gave her a gentle smile. 'I was a little scared to leave it, in case you came back and then left before I saw you. But in the end...'

'You came looking for me.'

'I ran the whole length of that lane, listening for the sound of your car starting up the whole time. And then, as I reached that clearing, I saw a flicker of movement by the willow tree—and stopped running. I was home—and with my love.'

'You knew, as we walked back to the top of that lane, that I was ready to bolt for it?'

Naylor nodded. 'I wasn't having that! And then, like music in my ears, I would swear, unless those ears are playing me false, there you are, sounding as ragingly jealous as I've felt, at the thought of me dating anyone but you.'

'It was a dead giveaway?'

'I wasn't that confident, but it was certainly something of a lifeline for me to cling on to—' He broke off. 'Are you going to allow me to kiss you yet?'

She wanted his kisses more than she could say. But perhaps, as he had suggested, she had been bruised by the happenings in her life. 'Is that everything? You haven't been devious about anything else?'

He did a swift mental recap. 'I fell in love with you—and had to hide it. Knew I had found my soul-mate—but you didn't want to know. I knew I had to see you again—but had to bide my time. While I couldn't be more pleased at the way things have turned out for Lewis and Eleanor, their getting to know each other has been a splendid opportunity for me to further my own cause—I've been prepared to use any angle I had to,' he confessed. 'I've telephoned you purely from a need to hear your voice—but had to pretend I was ringing to speak to Lewis, when I had already spoken to him at his home, when he had said it was just he and Eleanor there.'

'Last Saturday!' Romillie cried in surprise.

'I was going away. I needed to hear you before I went—I just hungered for the sound of your voice.'

'Oh, Naylor,' she whispered.

'So tell me,' he urged, taking heart from her tender tone, 'when did you first start to realise that you had feeling for me other than outright dislike?'

It was then that she knew she could not hold back any more, did not *want* to hold back, and in fact found that she would not hold back any more. That she, in fact, trusted him. For all he had been devious, his only deviousness had been because of his love for her.

'I think I've been a little devious too, in my pride to not let you see how my feelings for you were changing.'

'Then you understand my actions? Why I did what I have done, why I've behaved the way I've behaved.' He paused. 'You, my darling, you trust me?'

'Yes,' she said simply and, meeting halfway, they kissed.

And for long, long moments Naylor held her close up to him, before leaning back to look lovingly into her eyes. He kissed her again—but still wanted to know, 'When?'

'Quite early on, I think,' Romillie replied honestly. 'I

remember feeling just a touch put out that night we met that you barely seemed to notice me.'

He gave a delicious grin. 'I was overwhelmingly aware of you the whole while,' he replied.

'My love for you had been growing in my heart without me being aware of it,' she confessed. 'Then, when I knew I'd been sleepwalking and how you had looked out for me, had been protecting me, I knew that I was in love with you.'

'Sweet darling,' Naylor breathed. 'I hope you'll give me the right to protect you always.'

'That sounds—nice.' She had been going to say *That sounds permanent*, but she had a feeling Naylor did not mean it that way.

But then discovered that she was wrong about that when, looking directly into her liquid brown eyes, he began softly, 'You said you wanted to buy back that sketch?'

'I didn't think you truly wanted it.'

'Oh, but I did. Not from any sense of voyeurism,' he quickly assured her. 'Even though you do have such a beautiful body I was certain that no one else was going to own that drawing. And while I agree I wanted to eliminate every cause of stress that might cause you to walk in your sleep, in this case obviate the need for you to sell the family car, I had to have that drawing because it was so pure. Eleanor had somehow managed to capture so much of you—the honesty in your soul, your true smile—not the false one you favoured me with too many times— the inner beauty of you that shines out from your eyes.' He stopped, then went on, 'I'm afraid, my darling, I'm unable to sell it to you, but if you're willing I'll happily share it with you.'

'Me have it for six months and you have it for six months, do you mean?' She could not think what else he meant, but realised she must be wrong when even before she had finished, he was shaking his head.

'I'm sorry, Romillie, but that sketch stays with me.'

'I'm not sure I know…' *I'm not sure I know what you mean,*

174 HER HAND IN MARRIAGE

she would have said. But suddenly she thought she did know
what he meant—and flushed scarlet. 'You want to move in
with me?' She made a stab at it, but flushed again, knowing
straight away that she had got it wrong. 'I'm sorry,' she said in
a rush. 'I'm a bit confused,' she excused the conclusion she had
jumped to. 'I got it wrong…'

'Only slightly.' Naylor immediately put her out of her
misery. 'While I most definitely want us to live together, I was
thinking more in terms of you moving in to live here, with me.'

She stared at him, her heart racing. 'I…' she managed,
floundering. This was all so sudden, all so unexpected. And yet
she loved him with all her being.

'I know I'm asking a great deal of you, my dearest Romillie,'
Naylor said softly. 'But while I know that you'd brook no dishonesty or any underhandedness in any relationship we have,
you have to know too that neither will I.' He took a long breath,
and then, looking directly into her wide brown eyes, 'Which is
why, when I know you are totally against marriage, I have to
tell you, Romillie mine, that I will settle for nothing less.'

Shock, pure and simple, made her jerk back from him.
'You—want…?' she gasped.

'Don't be alarmed,' he urged, and held on to her quietly for
a few soothing seconds before, a hand going to his pocket, he
drew out a small jeweller's box. He opened it to reveal the most
exquisite diamond solitaire. 'Just wear this for a week or two
while you get used to the idea,' he encouraged gently, taking
the ring from its box.

She stared at it, her heart thundering. 'Where did you get it?'
she asked—rather inanely, she thought.

Though Naylor did not seem to think her question inane, but
answered, 'I saw it some while ago and thought, hoped, you
might like it.'

'You bought it—for me?' She was still having the utmost difficulty in taking this in.

'Only for you,' he answered, and, taking hold of her left hand, he slipped the ring on to her engagement finger.

'It—fits,' she murmured huskily.

'My darling, I have to tell you—we're engaged,' Naylor said tenderly, and gently kissed her.

Romillie's eyes were still huge in her face when he pulled back to look at her. 'But—but—you don't want to get married,' she protested, with what breath she had left.

'That, sweet love, was probably my biggest deception of all. I've known I wanted to marry you, to have you as my wife, from the moment I saw you.' Her eyes were saucer-wide as he went on, 'Just as I've known from the beginning that you would run a mile at the very thought of marrying anyone. Yet that Sunday morning here—you may remember it—we kissed in my bed and you were so irresistible I never wanted to stop kissing you. Then you said, "You know you're going to have to marry me," and I was so over my head about you I very nearly told you that to marry you had been my plan all along.'

She stared at him, believing yet disbelieving. 'But—you didn't! As I recall it, you were quite sharp in letting me know just what you thought about that notion.'

'Camouflage, pure and simple,' he owned. 'I realised that the moment to declare my true feelings for you was not right.'

She smiled, *could* smile now, as she recalled, 'So you decided to give me the aloof treatment?'

'You're pretty good at that yourself, as *I* recall,' he replied. 'But all that went by the board when Lewis got ill, and you and your mother rushed to the hospital.'

'It was a panicky few hours all round,' she agreed with a smile. And felt a need to kiss him. It was some while before Naylor let her go.

'So there we were,' he picked up, as though he too was striving to recall where they were. 'There's a glorious pink glow on your lovely face, by the way.' She laughed, which seemed to delight him, so that he had to kiss her again before manfully drawing back to recollect, 'And the next thing I know we're in my London apartment and you're suggesting we share my bed.'

'Was I so very forward?'

'Not you. But even so I knew I should not take you up on the offer. But hell, Romillie, I'd ached to have you near, ached with a constant yearning to have you close—and I—just couldn't resist the temptation to not have to part from you.'

'It was all pretty wonderful,' she remembered dreamily.

'Wasn't it, though?' he agreed tenderly.

'Well,' she qualified, 'it was up until that point where you said you would have to consider marrying me—and I knew then, as good as if you'd actually said it, that you meant the exact opposite, and that there was no way you would *think* of marrying me. It—um—hurt.'

'Oh, darling,' he murmured, and held her close for long moments before moving to look into her eyes. 'Do I take it from that that your views of marriage have undergone something of quite a dramatic change?'

She nodded. 'They started to—that weekend I stayed here,' she confessed, and was tenderly kissed for her confession.

'I'm sorry I hurt you, little one,' Naylor soothed. 'I didn't mean to. I suppose, if anything, I was testing the water, trying to gauge your feelings.' He smiled as he revealed, 'I thought I had my answer when you left the bed as though shot, telling me how I certainly knew how to kill the moment.'

'I'm sorry.' She was the one to apologise.

Naylor held her close again. 'I'm sorry too. I was a bear after that. But I've been so up and down over you—up one minute, when you were so pleased that Eleanor had agreed to marry Lewis, wondering if you'd changed your views on marriage. Down the next, when I realised marriage was fine for other people—but not for you. I tried to keep away from you. Work helped. Working in overdrive in order to get up to speed doing Lewis's work and most of mine. But even then I'm looking for reasons to contact you. I decided to put that ring in a drawer and forget about it. Only…'

'Only you saw me today and—' She broke off, staring at him as something suddenly struck her. 'That's why you went upstairs to change! You went to get this ring?'

He grinned, the most wonderful grin. 'You were here, where I wanted you to be. I reasoned you wouldn't have come anywhere near Oaklands if you absolutely hated me. You certainly wouldn't have gone wandering down to that stream if that spot wasn't just a tiny bit special to you too. And, unless I was clutching too desperately at straws, that had definitely been a note of outraged jealousy in your voice when you accused me of having a heavy date tonight. Quite honestly, little love, it seemed to me that the time had come for me to tell you how it is with me, and to find out what my chances were with you.' Tenderly he raised her left hand to his lips and kissed it. And, raising his head from the ring on her engagement finger to look deeply into her eyes, 'This is a small token of my love. Tell me, Romillie, is it going to stay on your finger?'

She looked back at him, her heart singing. 'Yes,' she said huskily—and thought he might kiss her. But he did not.

Searching intently into her lovely brown eyes, he asked, 'And will you, one day very soon, allow me to partner it by placing a plain band of gold on that same finger?'

She swallowed, feeling all choked-up suddenly. 'Yes,' she whispered. And still he did not kiss her.

But, as if needing to be sure that she understood what he was truly asking, asked solemnly, 'You'll marry me, Romillie Fairfax?'

She did not hesitate. 'Yes, Naylor Cardell, I would very much like to marry you,' she replied.

With a heartfelt sigh, Naylor drew her close up to his heart. 'My darling,' he breathed.

And then it was that he kissed her.

* * * * *

_Love Inspired_
# HISTORICAL

_Powerful, engaging stories of romance, adventure and faith
set in the past—when life was simpler and faith played a
major role in everyday lives._

_Turn the page for a sneak preview of_
_THE BRITON_
_by_
_Catherine Palmer_

_Love Inspired Historical—love and faith
throughout the ages
A brand-new line from Steeple Hill Books
Launching this February!_

"Welcome to the family, Briton," said one of Olaf's men in a mocking voice. "We look forward to the presence of a woman at our hall."

Bronwen grasped her tunic and yanked it from the Viking's thick fingers. As she stepped away from the table, she heard the drunken laughter of the barbarians behind her. How could her father have betrothed her to the old Viking?

Running down the stone steps toward the heavy oak door that led outside from the keep, Bronwen gathered her mantle about her. She ordered the doorman to open the door, and he did so reluctantly, pressing her to carry a torch. But Bronwen pushed past him and fled into the darkness.

Dashing down the steep, pebbled hill toward the beach, she felt the frozen ground give way to sand. She threw off her veil and circlet and kicked away her shoes.

Racing alongside the pounding surf, she felt hot tears of anger and shame well up and stream down her cheeks. With no concern for her safety, Bronwen ran and ran—her long braids streaming behind her, falling loose, drifting like a tattered black flag.

Blinded with weeping, she did not see the dark form that sprang up in her path and stopped dead her headlong sprint. Bronwen shrieked in surprise and fear as iron arms pinned her, and a heavy cloak threatened to suffocate her.

"Release me!" she cried. "Guard! Guard, help me."

"Hush, my lady." A deep voice emanated from the darkness. "I mean you no harm. What demon drives you to run through the night without fear for your safety?"

"Release me, villain! I am the daughter—"

"I shall hold you until you calm yourself. We had heard there were witches in Amounderness, but I had not thought to meet one so openly."

Still held tight in the man's arms, Bronwen drew back and peered up at the hooded figure. "You! You are the man who spied on our feast. Release me at once, or I shall call the guard upon you."

The man chuckled at this and turned toward his companions, who stood in a group nearby. Bronwen caught hold of the back of his hood and jerked it down to reveal a head of glossy raven curls. But the man's face was shrouded in darkness yet, and as he looked at her, she could not read his expression.

"So you are the blessed bride-to-be." He returned the hood to his head. "Your father has paired you with an interesting choice."

Relieved that her captor did not appear to be a highwayman, she pushed away from him and sagged onto the wet sand. "Please leave me here alone. I need peace to think. Go on your way."

The tall stranger shrugged off his outer mantle and wrapped it around her shoulders. "Why did your father betroth you thus to the aged Viking?" he asked.

"For one purported to be a spy, you know precious little about Amounderness. But I shall tell you, as it is all common knowledge."

She pulled the cloak tightly about her, reveling in its warmth. "This land, known as Amounderness, once was Briton territory. Olaf Lothbrok, my betrothed, came here as a youth when the Viking invasions had nearly subsided. He took the lands directly to the south of Rossall Hall from their Briton lord.

Then, of course, the Normans came, and Amounderness was pillaged by William the Conqueror's army."

The man squatted on the sand beside Bronwen. He listened with obvious interest as she continued. "When William took an account of Amounderness in his Domesday Book, he recorded no remaining lords and few people at all. But he did not know the Britons. Slowly we crept out of hiding and returned to our halls. My father's family reoccupied Rossall Hall. And there we live, as we should, watching over our serfs as they fish and grow their meager crops. Indeed, there is not much here for the greedy Normans to want, if they are the ones for whom you spy."

Unwilling to continue speaking when her heart was so heavy, Bronwen stood and turned toward the sea. The traveler rose beside her and touched her arm. "Olaf Lothbrok's lands—together with your father's—will reunite most of Amounderness under the rule of the son you are beholden to bear. A clever plan. Your sister's future husband holds the rest of the adjoining lands, I understand."

"You've done your work, sir. Your lord will be pleased. Who is he—some land-hungry Scottish baron? Or have you forgotten that King Stephen gave Amounderness to the Scots, as a trade for their support in his war with Matilda? I certainly hope your lord is not a Norman. He would be so disappointed to learn he has no legal rights here. Now, if you will excuse me?"

Bronwen turned and began walking back along the beach toward Rossall Hall. She felt better for her run, and somehow her father's plan did not seem so far-fetched anymore. Distant lights twinkled through the fog that was rolling in from the west, and she suddenly realized what a long way she had come.

"My lady," the man's voice called out behind her.

Bronwen kept walking, unwilling to face again the one who had seen her in her humiliation. She didn't care what he reported to his master.

"My lady, you have quite a walk ahead of you." The

traveler strode forward to join her. "I shall accompany you to your destination."

"You leave me no choice, I see."

"I am not one to compromise myself, dear lady. I follow the path God has set before me and none other."

"And just who are you?"

"I am called Jacques."

"French. A Norman, as I had suspected."

The man chuckled. "Not nearly as Norman as you are Briton."

As they approached the fortress, Bronwen could see that the guests had not yet begun to disperse. Perhaps no one had missed her, and she could slip quietly into bed beside Gildan.

She turned to go, but he took her arm and studied her face in the moonlight. Then, gently, he drew her into the folds of his hooded cloak. "Perhaps the bride would like the memory of a younger man's embrace to warm her," he whispered.

Astonished, Bronwen attempted to remove his arms from around her waist. But she could not escape his lips as they found her own. The kiss was soft and warm, melting away her resistance like the sun upon the snow. Before she had time to react, he was striding back down the beach.

Bronwen stood stunned for a moment, clutching his woolen mantle about her. Suddenly she cried out, "Wait, Jacques! Your mantle!"

The dark one turned to her. "Keep it for now," he shouted into the wind. "I shall ask for it when we meet again."

\* \* \* \* \*

Don't miss this deeply moving story,
THE BRITON,
available February 2008
from the new Love Inspired Historical line.

And also look for
HOMESPUN BRIDE
by Jillian Hart,
where a Montana woman discovers that love
is the greatest blessing of all.

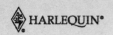

# HARLEQUIN®

# EVERLASTING LOVE™

*Every great love has a story to tell*™

# *The Valentine Gift*

## featuring
## three deeply emotional
## stories of love that stands
## the test of time, just in time
## for Valentine's Day!

*USA TODAY* bestselling author
## Tara Taylor Quinn

## Linda Cardillo

### and

## Jean Brashear

Available just in time for Valentine's Day
February wherever you buy books.

**www.eHarlequin.com**

HEL65427

# Silhouette® Desire

**NEW YORK TIMES BESTSELLING AUTHOR**

# DIANA PALMER

A brand-new Long, Tall Texans novel

## IRON COWBOY

*Available March 2008
wherever you buy books.*

# REQUEST YOUR FREE BOOKS!
## 2 FREE NOVELS PLUS 2
# FREE GIFTS!

## HARLEQUIN ROMANCE®

### From the Heart, For the Heart

**YES!** Please send me 2 FREE Harlequin Romance® novels and my 2 FREE gifts. After receiving them, if I don't wish to receive any more books, I can return the shipping statement marked "cancel." If I don't cancel, I will receive 4 brand-new novels every month and be billed just $3.57 per book in the U.S., or $4.05 per book in Canada, plus 25¢ shipping and handling per book and applicable taxes, if any*. That's a savings of over 15% off the cover price! I understand that accepting the 2 free books and gifts places me under no obligation to buy anything. I can always return a shipment and cancel at any time. Even if I never buy another book from Harlequin, the two free books and gifts are mine to keep forever.

114 HDN EEV7   314 HDN EEWK

| | |
|---|---|
| Name | (PLEASE PRINT) |
| Address | Apt. |
| City | State/Prov.     Zip/Postal Code |

Signature (if under 18, a parent or guardian must sign)

### Mail to the **Harlequin Reader Service®**:
**IN U.S.A.:** P.O. Box 1867, Buffalo, NY 14240-1867
**IN CANADA:** P.O. Box 609, Fort Erie, Ontario L2A 5X3

Not valid to current Harlequin Romance subscribers.

### Want to try two free books from another line?
### Call 1-800-873-8635 or visit www.morefreebooks.com.

\* Terms and prices subject to change without notice. NY residents add applicable sales tax. Canadian residents will be charged applicable provincial taxes and GST. This offer is limited to one order per household. All orders subject to approval. Credit or debit balances in a customer's account(s) may be offset by any other outstanding balance owed by or to the customer. Please allow 4 to 6 weeks for delivery.

**Your Privacy:** Harlequin is committed to protecting your privacy. Our Privacy Policy is available online at www.eHarlequin.com or upon request from the Reader Service. From time to time we make our lists of customers available to reputable firms who may have a product or service of interest to you. If you would prefer we not share your name and address, please check here. □

HR07

The second book in the deliciously passionate
Heart trilogy by *New York Times* bestselling author

# KAT MARTIN

As a viscount's daughter, vivacious Coralee Whitmore
is perfectly placed to write about London's elite in the
outspoken ladies' gazette *Heart to Heart*. But beneath her
fashionable exterior beats the heart of a serious journalist.

So when her sister's death is dismissed as suicide, Corrie vows
to uncover the truth, suspecting that the notorious Earl of
Tremaine was Laurel's lover and the father of her illegitimate
child. But Corrie finds the earl is not all he seems…nor is
she immune to his charms, however much she despises his
caddish ways.

"The first of [a] new series,
*Heart of Honor* is a grand
way for the author to begin…
Kat Martin has penned
another memorable tale."
—Historical Romance Writers

*Heart of Fire*

*Available the first week of January 2008
wherever paperbacks are sold!*

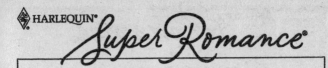

# Texas Hold 'Em

### When it comes to love, the stakes are high

Sixteen years ago, Luke Chisum dated
Becky Parker on a dare…before going
on to break her heart. Now the former
River Bluff daredevil is back, rekindling
desire and tempting Becky to pick up
where they left off. But this time she has
to resist or Luke could discover the secret
she's kept locked away all these years….

*Look for*

# TEXAS BLUFF

### *by* *Linda Warren*
#### #1470

*Available February 2008*
*wherever you buy books.*

# Coming Next Month

**Ranchers, lords, sheikhs and playboys—the perfect men
to make you sigh this Valentine's Day, from Harlequin Romance®...**

### #4003 CATTLE RANCHER, SECRET SON Margaret Way

Have you ever fallen in love at first sight? Gina did—but she knew she
could never be good enough for Cal's society family. Now Cal's determined
to marry her—but is it to avoid a scandal and claim his son, or because he
really loves her?

### #4004 RESCUED BY THE SHEIKH Barbara McMahon
*Desert Brides*

Be swept away to the swirling sands and cool oases of the Moquansaid
desert. Lost and alone, Lisa is relieved to be rescued by a handsome
stranger. But this sheikh is no ordinary man, and Lisa suddenly begins to
feel out of her depth again....

### #4005 THE PLAYBOY'S PLAIN JANE Cara Colter

You know the type: confident, sexy, gorgeous—and he knows it.
Entrepreneur Dylan simply has *it*. But Katie's no pushover and is
determined to steer clear—that is until she starts to see a side of him she
never knew existed.

### #4006 HER ONE AND ONLY VALENTINE Trish Wylie

Do you find yourself hoping for a special surprise on Valentine's Day?
Single mom Rhiannon's about to get a big one! When Kane left, breaking
Rhiannon's heart, he didn't know he'd left behind something infinitely
precious. But now he's back in town....

### #4007 ENGLISH LORD, ORDINARY LADY Fiona Harper
*By Royal Appointment*

It's so important to be loved for who you *really* are inside. Josie agrees,
and thinks new boss Will doesn't look beneath the surface enough. But
appearances can be deceptive, especially when moonlit kisses in the
castle orchard get in the way!

### #4008 EXECUTIVE MOTHER-TO-BE Nicola Marsh
*Baby on Board*

Career-girl Kristen's spontaneous decision to share one special night with
sexy entrepreneur Nathan was crazy—and totally out of character! But
now there are two shocks in store—one unexpected baby and one sexy
but very familiar new boss....

HRCNM0108